MW01128321

Then came the ultimate theme park

JESUS WORLD

A Prophetic Novel

Jamie Buckingham

www.JamieBuckinghamMinistries.com

Risky Living Ministries, Inc.

*Dedicated to reproducing and promoting
the life works of Jamie Buckingham*

LIKE us on
Facebook!

RLM, Inc.   e-mail
3901 Hield Road, NW   Bruce@rlmin.com
Palm Bay, FL 32907

Jesus World

Jamie Buckingham

Jesus World
By Jamie Buckingham

Published by Risky Living Ministries, Inc.
3901 Hield Road NW
Palm Bay, Florida, 32907
www.rlmin.com

Risky Living Ministries is dedicated to reproducing and
promoting the life's works of Jamie Buckingham.

ISBN: 978-1495369322

Cover Design by Bruce Buckingham

ABOUT JAMIE BUCKINGHAM

A master story-teller and Bible student, Jamie Buckingham has delighted millions around the world both in person and in print.

He wrote more than 45 books, including biographies of some of this century's best known Christians, including Pat Robertson (*Shout it From the Housetops*), Corrie ten Boom (*Tramp for the Lord* and others), and Kathryn Kuhlman (*Daughter of Destiny, God Can Do it Again* and others). His other biographies include the national best seller *Run Baby Run* (with Nicky Cruz), *From Harper Valley to the Mountaintop* (with Jeannie C. Riley), and *O Happy Day* (the Happy Goodman Family singers). Other books by Jamie Buckingham include *Risky Living, Into the Glory* (about the jungle aviators branch of Wycliffe Bible Translators); *Where Eagles Soar* (a sequel to *Risky Living*); *A Way Through the Wilderness*; *Coping with Criticism*; and *The Truth Will Set You Free--But First it Will Make You Miserable* (a collection of Jamie's wit and wisdom). He also wrote *Power for Living*, a book sponsored by the Arthur DeMoss Foundation that was given away to millions of people worldwide and resulted in untold numbers of people coming to Christ.

Jamie was more than an author of books. He was an award-winning columnist for *Charisma Magazine* and served as Editor-in-Chief of *Ministries Today Magazine* until his death in February of 1992.

A popular conference speaker, he was recognized as one of America's foremost authorities on the Sinai and Israel. He wrote and produced more than 100 video teachings on location in the Holy Land.

Jamie's books, columns, additional writings, video devotional series, and audio sermons can be found at www.JamieBuckinghamMinistries.com.

As a distinguished Bible teacher with graduate degrees in English Literature and Theology, Jamie was respected among liturgical, evangelical, and Pentecostal Christians. He was considered a close friend and confidant of many key Christians of the late 20th century, including Oral Roberts, Billy Graham, Catherine Marshall, Jack Hayford, Bob Mumford, Kathryn Kuhlman, Corrie ten Boom, John Sherrill, Bill Bright, Bernie May, John Hagee, Pat Robertson, and many others.

Most importantly, Jamie was a husband, father, grandfather, and founding pastor of the Tabernacle Church, an interdenominational congregation in Melbourne, Florida, where he served for 25 years, pastoring and discipling followers of Christ. He lived in a rural area on the east coast of Florida on a family compound with his wife, Jackie, surrounded by five married children and 14 grandchildren.

For more information on Jamie Buckingham, his life and his ministry, please visit www.JamieBuckinghamMinistries.com

Jesus World

DEDICATION

There are few real persons left in our world. Even in the Kingdom so many are made of plastic. Mickey Evans, though, is real.

To the ranchers and farmers around Lake Okeechobee in Florida he is pastor, counselor and friend.

To the cowboys, as he saddles his horse and rides beside them in their loneliness, he is the reality of God.

To the prisoners in the jails, he is a way of life.

To the alcoholics who become part of the family at Dunklin Memorial Camp in the wilderness between Indiantown and Okeechobee, he is boss and teacher.

To me ... Mickey Evans is a breath of fresh air in a world full of robots. He is a man willing to think small enough to make his vision come to pass.

He is my friend.

Thanks, Mickey, for not trying to improve on the methods of Jesus.

-- Jamie Buckingham

Jesus World

PROLOGUE

It was a perfect day for the Crucifixion. The temperature was in the lower 80s. The azure blue sky was dotted with white, fluffy clouds. The orange blossoms from the surrounding groves perfumed the air.

By ten in the morning there were already 65,000 people in the park. It was to be a record-breaking day, with Jesus World sure to outdraw both the Tampa Bay Bucs and Miami Dolphins, professional football teams.

The procession began at noon from a stage door on the Via Dolorosa, the robot Jesus at the head carrying his cross. Slowly he moved from the bottom of Calvary to the summit. Soft music from speakers in the bushes set the somber mood and the spectators were hushed. Soldiers approached the robot Jesus and threw him to the ground, then lay him on the cross. Nails were driven into his hands and feet. Then the cross was raised.

The earth roared and shook from immense under-ground vibrators. Styrofoam stones toppled from the walls. The veil of the Temple was split.

The figure on the cross sagged....

Jesus World

I

THE SEA WAS SPARKLING GREEN, shimmering in the midday tropical sun. The white prow of the big yacht, now slowed from full power, sliced easily through the transparent water, leaving a trail of foam and bubbles behind.

High on the flying bridge Simon Pedersen, his right hand on the twin throttles, eased back on the controls. The water here was shallow, less than two fathoms, and Pedersen did not want to chance scraping the bottom of his 58-foot yacht, *Marah,* on the rocks below.

Just ahead was Grand Bahama Island and the harbor at West End. The lean, tanned captain loved the feel of the salt spray on his face. His shirt was open, exposing the curly, silver hair matted across his bronzed chest -- glistening with the salt of sweat and sea. His firm face and muscular arms disguised the fact he was the head of one of America's largest financial empires.

It had been a rough ride across from Ft. Pierce, Florida -- the kind of ride Pedersen enjoyed. It took him back to his early teens, fighting the North Sea off the coast of Norway in his stepfather's fishing boats. This time the seas had been running eight feet in the Gulf Stream, causing the waves to break over the bow and splash against the Plexiglas windscreen on the high bridge. But now on the lee side of the big island the water was like glass. All the details of the bottom-the starfish, the brilliant conch shells and the occasional coral banks -- were visible as the big boat glided over the surface, moving slowly as the depth finder spotted the ever-shifting channel.

Pedersen turned and grinned at his single passenger, a stocky man who was standing beside him on the bridge.

"Feel better?" Pedersen chuckled.

Bert Jessup nodded his head slightly. His face was still a pale green from the intense vomiting he had experienced only an hour before. But now, as the big yacht glided through the smooth water near the harbor, his strength seemed to be returning.

Bert Jessup, one of the nation's best known evangelists, had something on his mind. He had made the trip from Florida to the Bahamas several times aboard the *Marah.* Always before it had been with invited guests -- men and women who wanted to know more about God. But this time Jessup wanted to talk only to his wealthy friend, Simon Pedersen.

Simon was Jessup's strongest supporter. The head of one of the nation's largest hotel conglomerates, owner of America's second largest newspaper syndicate, Vox Populi, he was in many respects Bert's closest friend. It was Pedersen who had let Bert Jessup use -- free of charge -- the 20 acres where his Jesus World Ministries headquarters were located. Pedersen owned 2500 acres close by Walt Disney World near Orlando, and the prime section was where Jessup's Jesus World was located. The men had been friends many years.

Jessup's intense phone call to Simon two days before had intrigued the businessman, however. The evangelist was not given to "visions," and when he used that word over the phone, Simon agreed to fly down from Chicago immediately. The next morning the two men were aboard the yacht heading for the Bahamas.

Ahead was the entrance to the marina. Pedersen pulled down on the twin controls to the left of the wheel. The engines reversed, bringing the big boat to a standstill in the transparent water. A clumsy sailboat was coming through the long, canal-like entrance to the marina. Pedersen waited until it cleared the jetties and turned toward the open sea. He pushed the throttles forward. Deep in the hold the mighty twin turbo diesels rumbled back to life. The yacht slipped through the narrow channel and into the crowded marina.

Twenty times during the seven years he had known Bert Jessup, Pedersen had made the run to the Bahamas in the *Marah*. He loved it when he pushed the throttles forward and felt the big yacht leap forward "on the step," slicking through the deep blue waters of the Gulf Stream.

Standing on the flying bridge, his radar screen gave him a picture of what he could not see with his naked eye. The bank of powerful electronics in the lockers under the wheel kept him in touch with land and other boats. Years before he had promised Jessup to use the yacht as a place of ministry. To Simon Pedersen, the "Silver Fisherman" as his men called him, the boat belonged to God.

He guided the three-story yacht into the marina at West End, spotting his slip. He maneuvered the big boat like a child pushing a toy car across the carpet. Standing with his back to the wheel, he faced the stern, his hands behind him on the controls. Shifting the engines expertly from port to starboard, reversing first one engine then the other, he gently slipped the boat between the barnacle-covered pilings.

Cutting the throttles, he shouted to his passenger.

"Tie off the bow, Bert. I'll get the stem lines."

The stocky man ran forward, slipping on the wet deck, grabbing for the coiled lines. After several unsuccessful attempts, he finally threw the heavy loop around one of the big pilings. Sweating from the slight exertion in the hot sun, he bent over and tied the other end to the bow hitch. Then he ran to the other side of the bow and repeated the maneuver.

In the meantime, Simon Pedersen had already finished with his stem lines and was busy folding his charts in the cockpit.

A tall Bahamian approached down the dock, his starched white uniform contrasting with the black of his face and arms.

"How was the trip over, Cap'n?" the immigration officer grinned.

"High seas, clear skies, and the presence of the Almighty."

"A man cannot ask for more," the black man smiled broadly.

"Only one passenger this time," Pedersen said as he finished folding the charts and stuffed them in his briefcase. "I'll fill out the cards and bring them to your office."

The officer hesitated

"Oh yes," Pedersen chuckled, running his hands through his thick, silver hair. "I have those things you asked me to bring."

The officer beamed in appreciation as Pedersen opened an ice chest at the back of the boat and handed the man several packages of frozen meat and American canned goods -- things the officer had requested for his family the last time the *Marah* left West End for the States. The two men shook hands like old friends.

Simon finished hooking up the fresh water and power from the fixtures on the dock. Then he turned and surveyed the marina. It was almost full of boats -- some small, some large -- but the *Marah* remained the queen of the Caribbean.

Fully air-conditioned with cabins fore and aft, two full bathrooms (heads) and a half bath with a lavatory and toilet, complete with galley and the sleeping space for twelve, she was as fancy as any hotel in the Pedersen chain.

It was Jessup, several years before, who had suggested a new use for the yacht "Both of us have influential friends -- hungry for spiritual things -- who would enjoy an excursion in the Bahamas," he said "You have business connections. I have people who are attracted because of my TV program. We can feed them fresh lobster, conch fritters, fresh red snapper and grouper -- then talk to them about faith."

Although Simon did not consider himself a church man, he had become a believer through the influence of his Norwegian stepfather, a giant of a fisherman who had once told him that Jesus' choice of a pulpit was a fishing boat.

Jessup's suggestion that he invite small groups aboard the *Marah* reminded him of his father's words. Under Bert's guidance Simon had learned to communicate the gospel in relaxed settings.

Simon had been surprised by the results. His

guests had been receptive to Scripture, engrossed by
the Man who walked sandy beaches, proclaiming
Himself a fisher of men. Several lives had been
turned around, including a U.S. senator, the current
Secretary of Labor, a president of one of the
nation's largest corporations, several movie actors,
and three tough newspaper editors and publishers
connected with Vox Populi. Pedersen soon dubbed
the excursions the "fishers of men" cruises.

Bert Jessup lost interest in the cruises after
attending the first few. He admitted his primary
interest was in reaching the masses. His weekly TV
program, originating from the beautiful grounds of
Jesus World Ministries headquarters, brought
thousands of responses each week. In his city wide
crusades and his overseas campaigns, he had
reached millions. Aside from Billy Graham, few
men in this century had been as successful with
mass evangelism as Bert Jessup.

On this trip Jessup, despite his seasickness, was
more intense than Simon had ever seen him.
Halfway over from Florida, when the seas were
crashing against the windscreen and the boat was
rolling wildly, Simon had glanced over at his
passenger to see how he was doing.

"Do you want to turn back," he had shouted
above the roar of the engines and the crashing of the
sea.

"The fire in my bones is greater than the nausea
in my stomach," Jessup had shouted back gamely.

Simon left the immigration cards at the office
at the end of the dock. Then the two men ate dinner
in the dining room of the Grand Bahama Hotel,
which was within walking distance of the marina.

Simon sat across the table looking at the
evangelist, whose sunburned face was now showing

the effects of four hours in the blistering sun. Jessup was seven years younger than the wealthy businessman. Short, stocky, his brown hair was now streaked with gray. Many religious prognosticators, especially those with Vox Populi, had indicated that Jessup was the heir apparent to Billy Graham.

Using the property donated by Pedersen, Jessup had developed the 20-acre tract not far from the entrance to Walt Disney World outside Orlando, Florida, into a beautiful garden spot attraction called Jesus World.

Here families could come and bathe in the Old World atmosphere of Jesus and His disciples. Wax figures decorated the beautiful "Garden of Gethsemane," which was designed in quiet, reverent taste. Sitting on stone benches under the spreading trees, or kneeling on the soft grass, hundreds of travelers each day found this to be a place of serenity and prayer amidst all the commercialism that surrounded central Florida. The garden also provided the beautiful set for Jessup's TV productions, Jesus World Ministries, videotaped several times each year.

Recently Bert had expanded Jesus World to include two scenes from the Old Testament. One was a pastoral setting with a wax figure of the shepherd boy, David, sitting on a rock, with a harp as though singing psalms. The other required a bit more landscaping, but it, too, was a simple, serene place. Jessup had designed a small garden around twelve springs (actually water directed from a deep artesian well which flowed over coquina rocks) where he had planted 70 palm trees. He called this place Elim after the oasis in the wilderness where the children of Israel found refreshment. Free of charge, weary tourists, tired of their sojourns through Walt Disney World, Sea World, Universal Studios and the other nearby attractions, could come to Jesus World to pray, meditate, and leave refreshed.

On the back side of Pedersen's property, accessible only by a dirt road, Simon had leased another 200 acres -- also free of charge -- to a cowboy preacher named Joe Panther who ran what he called a "discipleship training ranch." He named it Koinonia. Simon had met Panther only once, but the meeting had convinced him he should let the rancher, who was part Indian, use his property for his training school.

Actually, the introduction had come through Simon's old friend, the late Walt Disney. Disney had been in the process of building his Walt Disney World when he met Joe Panther. He was fascinated by Panther's work with the central Florida cowboys and urged Pedersen to let the cowboy preacher use the back 200 acres of his land -- which was mostly pasture anyway -- to build his ranch. Simon had never visited the ranch, although it had been in operation 18 years. But the reports he received from men like Jessup, who knew Joe Panther, were always good.

"It takes a special breed of man to work with cowboys," Bert had once told Simon, "especially drunk cowboys. Panther speaks their language. He preaches some at the cattle auctions, but his big thing is to put the men to work and teach them the Bible. He has a good ministry, but thank God I'm not called to do the same thing."

Thus, on the word of men like Jessup, Simon had been willing to let Koinonia Ranch use his property.

After dinner, Bert and Simon strolled across the

beautiful grounds of the hotel down to the beach. The moon was at half crescent, almost directly overhead. The beach was quiet. The men walked silently on the sand, listening to the water lapping against the beach. Far behind them a long pier extended out into the sea. At the end there was a huge stern-wheeler strung with gaudy light bulbs. Ahead of them in the darkness was the long stone jetty which bordered the entrance to the marina where they had entered that afternoon.

Among the coconut palms at the edge of the beach, a white girl, a guest of the hotel, sat talking to one of the black Bahamian porters. Pedersen broke the silence, nodding in the direction of the couple.

"These girls come to West End to gamble at the casino at Freeport and to pick up a Bahamian as an escort for the weekend. They're airline stewardesses, cocktail waitresses, real estate salesgirls, or recent divorcees. They look on this as a lark, a fling. The porters at the hotel give them a line -- the same line they gave to the girl last week, the same line they'll give to another girl next week. The girls know it's a lie, but it's better to hear someone say he loves you, even if you know it's a lie, than never to hear it at all."

Pedersen paused, his mind running back to his wife, Cynthia. He loved her deeply, but over the last several years they had drifted apart. Cynthia drank too much. When he had left the day before to fly to Florida, there had been a nasty argument over his constant traveling and inattention to her and their grown son, Mark.

Simon longed for the days when they had walked hand in hand on the beach. Now they could barely communicate.

The young couple, seeing the two men approach, got up from their place on the bench and, hand in hand, headed back toward the hotel.

"I wish there were some way I could tell kids like that how much more there is to life," Simon said quietly.

"That's what I want to talk to you about," Bert Jessup said. The two men turned and walked toward the bench which the couple had just vacated.

Pedersen waited. He knew Bert had something important on his mind. He also knew better than to push it. When the time came, Jessup would open up.

"I turned 40 this week," Bert began. "I've been preaching for 23 years. But the world is going to hell -- by the billions. I feel I've got to do something to turn the tide. Something big."

"Well, you're doing a lot more than most people," Pedersen replied. "You've got a nationwide TV show. Your newspaper column is read all over the country."

"Yes, thanks to Vox Populi," Jessup conceded. "You've helped me more than any man on earth. But time is running out. Communism is taking over the world. Islam is the fastest growing religion on earth -- with twice as many Muslim conversions each year as Christian. It's terrifying what's happening in Africa, the Orient, behind the Iron Curtain, and in nations like India and Ethiopia. So many of these nations used to be Christian -- now they're either Muslim or Communistic.

"And here at home secular humanism is running rampant. We can't pray in the schools; the only way Jesus Christ ever gets into a courtroom is when someone mutters 'so help me God'; our university system is saturated with humanism and

Jamie Buckingham

most of the large denominations are so liberal you can't even call them Christian anymore. Simon, this world is going to hell faster than we can blink our eyes. I've got to do something gigantic to swing the world to Jesus Christ."

He paused, then said movingly, "So that girls like the one who just left to spend the night with that hotel porter can know Jesus Christ."

"You mentioned some kind of vision over the phone?"

"Last Monday, on my 40th birthday, I gave my entire staff a vacation. We closed the office and closed our Jesus World attractions. The place was deserted. I spent all day alone on the grounds -- fasting, praying, seeking God's plan for my life. Just at dusk, as the sun was setting, I went over to the Garden of Gethsemane. I sat on one of the stone benches and began to cry. I thought of all the people who had come into that little garden, had sat on those benches, had seen those wax figures of Jesus and His disciples, and had left as empty as when they came in. I looked over at the wax figure of Jesus kneeling there beside the rock and literally screamed: 'Why can't you talk? Why do you have to be made out of wax?'

"Just then the fireworks went off at Disney World, on the other side of the Interstate. The entire sky lit up with the skyrockets. Simon, it was as clear an answer to prayer as I've ever experienced. Only one time before in my life have I felt the power of God as strongly -- and that was when I was called into the ministry on my 17th birthday."

"I don't understand," Simon said sincerely.

"You would have had to be there to catch the full impact. Here I am with my wax Jesus. Over there is Walt Disney World, drawing a million people a month. Jesus told His followers that 'the children of this world are in their generation wiser than the children of light.' As I was sitting here, looking at all those fireworks and weeping for the lost souls of the world, I heard words, as plainly spoken as your words to me. The words were: *Make to yourself friends of the mammon of unrighteousness.*

"Why should Walt Disney be more attractive than Jesus Christ? Why is it you can pick up a phone book and find any item you want in the yellow pages -- except salvation? It's not right for the children of this world to be wiser than the children of light. It's time for a man to arise who will shake this world to its core for Jesus. I believe God has called me to be that man."

Simon was leaning forward on the bench, listening intently. He knew very little about visions, prophecies, and calls from God. But he knew enough to realize the words Bert Jessup had spoken were from Scripture -- "Make to yourself friends of the mammon of unrighteousness." In fact, that was the same verse, from Luke 16, his Sunday school teacher in Chicago had used the week before. The teacher said it meant that Christians should use all the methods of the world to build the Kingdom of God. Simon had questioned it at the time, for he thought there was more to the verse than the teacher had quoted. But now, hearing it again just a few days later from his trusted friend, Bert Jessup, he was convinced God had spoken.

"I stayed in the Garden most of the night," Jessup said. "I had cried out for Jesus to speak -- and He did. The plans began to form in my mind so rapidly I had to race back to the office to get paper and pen and write them down before I forgot them. It was as if God was outlining the very blueprints for the evangelization of the world."

He paused, got up from the bench and suddenly whirled to face Pedersen. "You are part of that plan, Simon. God told me to speak to you. He has not only chosen me, He has chosen you. He needs you and those four square miles of land across from Disney World."

Simon sat, speechless, looking at the intense man now pacing back and forth on the sand in front of the bench.

"It will be Jesus World in capital letters. A hundred times bigger and more spectacular than Walt Disney ever dreamed. We will recreate the scenes of the Bible, we'll build a scale model of Herod's temple, we'll have holograms of Jesus walking on the water. And when they come -- by the millions -- they'll hear the Word of God. It will be Christianity's answer to communism, Islam, humanism. We'll make Jesus so attractive that children and grandparents alike will come from all over the world to see Him in *His world.* It will be so big, so electrifying, so exciting that nobody on earth will miss it."

"Bert, you know I'm not a theologian. I'm just a layman. I've supported your ministry because I believe there is a place for the evangelist. But the only work I've done for Jesus is to bring these small groups over here to the Bahamas on the *Marah.* At times I can almost picture Him aboard my boat, sitting on the fantail fishing, helping with the cooking when we're making conch fritters, sitting cross-legged on the beach under a moon like this, talking to a small group of men. My question is this, Bert: Has anyone ever improved on the methods of Jesus as He walked the shore of Galilee with a group of disciples?"

"You have only a small part of the big picture, Simon," Jessup said excitedly.

"You forget Jesus also spoke to crowds -- huge mobs. His miracles attracted thousands. And what about Pentecost? Look what happened there when all Jerusalem turned out to see what was going on. What Pentecost was to the early church, so Jesus World will be to the church today. This could even be the 'latter rain' the Bible speaks about before the final return of Jesus."

"That's pretty ambitious, Bert."

"I learned it from you, old friend," Jessup laughed. "Weren't you the one who said, 'Think big; God doesn't bless small plans.'"

Simon allowed a slow grin to spread over his bronzed face. He rose to his feet and stood for a long moment looking up at the moon, listening to the wind rustling the palm branches and the waves lapping the smooth beach.

"Bert, more than anything in the world I want to be in the will of God. But I'm a spiritual novice. I have to take my directions from men like you."

"Others may remain in the safety of the boat, Simon. But as for me, I believe Jesus has called me to do this thing -- this big thing. I'm ready to walk on water."

Simon's voice was pensive. "There are a lot of areas in my life where things aren't going well. Cynthia and I have drifted apart. She's jealous of the time I give to these cruises. She resents my business success. She resents me ...." Simon's voice trailed off.

Jessup sat down on the bench beside his friend,

his hand resting gently on the larger man's knee. His voice was gentle. "Simon, I believe with all my heart Cynthia will respond to a big commitment on your part. She thinks you're just playing little boy games on your boat. But when she sees you are committed to this vision for worldwide evangelism, when she sees you're not just coming down to Florida every once in a while on a holy junket, when she sees you have committed all you have to the cause of Christ, she'll catch the vision too. When she does, your marriage will be healed."

Simon sat silently, looking out past the end of the reef to the little island where the palm trees were silhouetted against the moonlit sky. Cynthia and Mark both resented him. Maybe Bert was right. If they saw how seriously he felt about God -- serious enough to consider giving away a piece of land worth many millions of dollars, serious enough to commit himself to the most extravagant evangelistic plan in history -- maybe things would be different.

Simon reached over and put his hand on top of Jessup's hand, which was still resting on his knee. "It's a huge gamble," he said quietly. "But if you say God drew up the plans and put me in them, I'd better give it serious consideration."

"I'll need more than the property, Simon," Bert said, his voice quivering with excitement "I'll need your business advice. I'll need your close association so I won't make mistakes. We're talking about the biggest ministry project in all history. It isn't just land and money I'll need, Simon. Give me yourself as well."

Simon had always thought big. Now Bert Jessup was pushing him to think bigger than he had ever done in his whole life.

II

THE LANDING LIGHTS of the sleek
Gulfstream jet picked out the black streaks on
the concrete runway as it hissed to a landing. It
was well after midnight and the suburbs of
Chicago were asleep. The private jet, silver with
the black outline of a leaping fish on the nose,
whined to a stop in front of the dimly lit hangar.
A security guard ran to the door to help lower the
steps. Behind him were the sprawling corporate
headquarters of Pedersen Enterprises.

Simon Pedersen was the first out of the
plane. Carrying his expensive briefcase, he
nodded at the guard and turned to wave goodbye
to his pilot. Simon was eager to get home to his
wife. He headed for the silver Mercedes parked
in the hangar.

Silver was Simon's color. In spite of his
position as head of one of the world's largest
conglomerates, he had never forgotten his
beginnings as a fisherman in Norway. Although
Pedersen Enterprises no longer owned a single
fishing boat, Simon still liked to keep the image
and smiled when the press referred to him as
"The Silver Fisherman."

He did everything he could to foster the image.
He was seldom seen in public in anything but black
and gray -- to accent his silver hair. Cynthia called
this egomania. "It's because you grew up poor," she
said "When you're born rich, as I was, you don't
need to show off as much."

Maybe she was right. Simon thought as he climbed into his diesel Mercedes. Although his chauffeur usually met him at the hangar, Simon had given him the night off since he was six hours late in arriving. He needed to get back to Cynthia as quickly as possible. He had called home several times before leaving Florida and received no answer. His hands were clammy as he turned the key in the ignition and waited for the red "glow plug" light on the dash to blink off so he could start his car.

The streets were deserted, and he pushed the accelerator to the floor. It would take him less than 20 minutes to reach the house, 12 miles away in the sleeping suburb of Wayne.

Cynthia had been drinking before he left two days before. They always argued when she was drinking, especially if it preceded one of Simon's out-of-town trips. Then she had dismissed the maid. Simon hated for her to be alone in that big house -- especially when she was depressed. He felt fear knotting in his stomach like a snarled ball of twine. He could feel little beads of perspiration forming on his upper lip.

If only Mark would stay home to look after his mother. But Mark couldn't be counted on. At 26 he was still a playboy, flying all over the world in one of the company's jets. Brilliant, with a Master in Business Administration from Harvard, he was wasting his intellect at the gaming tables in Las Vegas. Simon also suspected he was involved with cocaine. He had had things too easy. He needed responsibility. Maybe, Simon thought, he could involve him in the business affairs of Jesus World. That way he could see the reality of God firsthand.

Simon turned his car off the thoroughfare into

the wooded subdivision where he lived. Only an occasional street light illuminated the darkened lawns of the luxurious homes. He slowed down to go over the speed bumps in the street. Out there, in the corporate world, things were moving in high gear. But here, in Woodland Acres, the world slowed down.

But not Simon Pedersen. At 48 years of age, he felt he was just beginning to hit his stride. And now he was contemplating adding Jesus World to his list of activities. That could be the biggest work of all.

It make him think back to those difficult days of childhood, running with his mother, a German Jewess, just one step in front of the coming holocaust. They had fled north across Germany into Denmark. There friendly Danes smuggled the two of them across the North Sea to safety in Norway.

But the war quickly spread north to Scandinavia. The day before the Nazis marched into Norway, his mother married Thor Pedersen, a grizzled and craggy Norwegian fisherman who was old enough to be her father. Thor had seen little Simon playing on the docks and through him had met the young widow. The courtship had lasted only a few weeks. Then Thor's desire to protect the mother and child from the coming Nazis compelled him to marry her and change her Jewish name to Pedersen.

During the war years this strange trio literally lived aboard Thor's fishing boat. Despite the German restrictions, Thor, who was a giant of a man, continued to fish -- moving far to the north of the Arctic Circle and running his fishing boats in the fjords all the way from Tromso and Hammerfest in the summer to the southern waters in the winter. Some of Simon's fondest memories were of those days when his stepfather, a man with hands like fish traps, taught him everything he knew about the sea -- and about God. Even though his mother never renounced her Jewish faith, it was natural for Simon to become a Christian like his stepfather.

After Thor's death, Simon took over the fishing fleet -- and then moved to Boston. It was there he had met Cynthia. In a few short years he had built up the biggest independently owned fleet of fishing boats in the western hemisphere. In the early '60s he began to diversify. On a whim he bought the old Fairborn Hotel on Miami Beach, where his mother lived in a penthouse apartment until she died. Shortly afterwards Simon bought the Mayflower hotel chain. Then in a move that shocked the stock market, he then converted both chains into the Pedersen Inns which soon became known the world over from the lavishly decorated Bangkok Pedersen to the new 30-story hotel on the bank of the Nile in Cairo.

The hotels, however, were only a small portion of his vast financial empire. There were also International Camp Grounds, the newspaper syndicate, the huge banking interest in Switzerland, and the computer house in Belgium -- the world's largest. Each year Simon Pedersen had become richer and richer until even he did not know how much he was worth.

Yet all his increased wealth seemed to bring more tension. Mark's irresponsibility was a constant bone of contention between Simon and Cynthia. Simon felt Mark should accept the corporate challenge. Cynthia argued that the problem was Simon's hyperactivity, not Mark's laziness.

Though independently wealthy, the roots of her family tree entwined with the Cabots and Lodges in

Boston. Cynthia had a strange instability. She was
beautiful, outspoken, captivating, yet underneath
quite insecure about herself, needing constant
reassurance. Family wealth had produced in her a
lot of guilt which she tried to handle by sometimes
taking far-out positions. This rebelliousness was
one of the reasons she fell in love with Simon.
Cynthia thought it would shock her parents if she
married this tough young Norwegian fisherman
with the Jewish mother. In twenty-seven years of
marriage to Simon she had changed little. She
remained unstable, self-centered, capable, Simon
knew, of doing the extreme just to get her own way.

That was the reason Simon was afraid as he
pulled up the driveway of the huge white stucco
house, trimmed in oxblood-stained wood. The
architecture was a blend of Tudor and the Bavarian
houses he had remembered as a child in Germany --
the kind his poor Jewish parents never could afford.
The security guard at the front gate said there had
been no activity at the house since he had come on
duty at 7 p.m. He had assumed that Mrs. Pedersen
had retired early since there were no lights on in the
house. Only the outside floodlights, flickering
behind the trees, illuminated the house.

Simon pulled his car into the garage, relieved to
find Cynthia's Cadillac parked in the other space.
Behind him the door slid shut automatically. He
picked up his briefcase and entered the darkened
house.

Even though it was early summer, there was a
chill in the darkness. The only light was the dim
reflection of the floodlights through the shrouded
windows, casting eerie shadows on the walls.
Cynthia did not like live-in help. Simon wished now
he had insisted upon it as he felt for a light switch

on the wall. He clicked it twice, but the bulb in the lamp seemed to be burned out. Moving cautiously through the den, he kicked an object on the floor, heard it roll across the carpet and clink against the side of the brick hearth. He snapped on the floor lamp and stared at the object. It was a bottle. Empty.

He swore under his breath. It was bad enough for Cynthia to drink in bed, but to leave an empty bourbon bottle on the floor was inexcusable. He started for the front hall but paused again. There was something wrong. Something desperately wrong in the house. It was something he could feel rather than smell or hear. He felt a cold shudder run down his back. His throat was dry. He needed to get upstairs to Cynthia.

Coming out of the den into the dark front hall, he reached for the banister post to guide his way up the dimly lit stairs. Again he kicked something. This time it did not roll. Instead it gave before his foot He pushed again with his shoe. The object was soft -- and moved awkwardly. In the dim light he could see a form. He reached down and his fingers felt first the soft, flimsy material, then the cold, stiff flesh beneath it.

Gasping, he dropped to his knees. He still could not see clearly, but his hands quickly ran the length of a body.

"Dear God, no! Oh, no!" It was Cynthia.

He leaped for the light switch at the head of the stairs. In the blaze of the white light he could see her body. Grotesquely bent, one leg twisted up behind her back. She had been dead for hours, her head caught in the banister as she had fallen. Her neck was obviously broken.

III

SIMON PEDERSEN struggled to cope with Cynthia's death. Early the next morning, as his associates were trying to locate Mark, who had last been seen at the tables in Lake Tahoe, he called Bert Jessup.

"The doctor called it an accident," Simon said, his voice barely audible over the phone. "She had been dead for almost 24 hours. But I found the empty pill bottles upstairs. When they do the autopsy, they'll know, too."

Jessup tried to comfort Simon over the phone. "You mustn't blame yourself, Simon. Cynthia has been sick for a long time. You're not responsible for her actions."

But Simon barely heard the words. He was going through the agony of self-accusation. "What if I had stayed home? What if I had called earlier? What if…what if...?" Dimly he heard Jessup say he would catch the next plane for Chicago and conduct the private graveside services the following day. He thanked him and hung up, questions drumming against his brain.

Why had this happened?

Why had it happened just as he was about to make a new and life-changing commitment to God?

Was God testing him?

Or punishing him?

All that morning he sat alone at his desk in his paneled study. The servants were talking in whispers as they bustled through the big house. Members of his staff were busy on the telephones, trying to locate Mark, talking to the press, issuing news releases. But Simon, shrouded in guilt and grief, sat alone in his study with orders that he was to talk to no one.

He stared vacantly at the walls lined with pictures of the past. There was a yellowed photograph of Cynthia, then a budding debutante in Boston, standing on the deck of one of his fishing boats in Boston Harbor. There was Cynthia and teenaged Mark in front of the newly opened Mexicala Pedersen in Guadalajara. How tall and thin Mark looked, towering over his mother more than a foot. Even then he had a sullen expression on his face. There was a black and white photo of all the publishers who made up the original group of Vox Populi. The group was ten times that size now, but those were exciting days. He remembered how he was able to get the names of his hotels and businesses in all those family newspapers across the nation by giving favors to the editors. "There's no salesman as good as a bribed editor," he used to joke with his board.

"God," he thought, "as a Christian, what a phony I have been."

Hanging on the wall in the far comer was a photo of Simon, Cynthia, and Walt Disney in front of the Singapore Pedersen. Simon remembered the conversation that afternoon -- so many years before. Disney and Pedersen had gone on a private tour of the Singapore harbor. Cynthia, as usual, had opted to stay behind in the hotel with Mark, who was just a boy. Disney confided in Simon that he was planning on building a huge recreation complex -- Walt Disney World -- south of Orlando, Florida, near the

sleepy little cow town of Kissimmee. He urged
Pedersen to buy land that was available nearby.

So Pedersen had purchased the 2500 acres --
almost four square miles of pastureland. Across the
years the property had increased in value until now
it was worth hundreds of millions. Even back then
Simon had sensed the property would be used in
some special way. Part of that had been fulfilled in
the small plots leased to Jessup and to Joe Panther.
But he had always believed there was something
bigger in store: was it Jessup's new concept of Jesus
World?

Or did Cynthia's death mean his life should go
in a 'completely new direction?

Bert Jessup arrived early the next morning.
They had gone immediately into Simon's study and
Simon had taken his place in his desk chair. It was
then he found the note. It had obviously been there
all the time, written in Cynthia's beautiful script,
lying on the blotter in the middle of his polished
mahogany desk. He must have looked at it a dozen
times the day before, but somehow his eyes had not
seen it. But this time he saw it, folded neatly, with
just his name, "Simon," written on the outside.

Pedersen picked it up, slowly unfolded it, and
then he looked up at Jessup who was standing on
the far side of the desk. Simon's face was white,
drained of all color. His lips were quivering.

"I can't ..." he choked out.

He handed the note to Jessup, his hands
trembling. Bert began to read. Out loud:

*You can live without me. In fact, you've been
living without me for 15 years....*

"You don't need to hear this," Bert said gently,

starting to fold the note and put it in his pocket "This is a trick of the devil to upset you just before the funeral."

Pedersen looked up, his eyes rimmed with red, his face haggard "Bert, all my life I have lived a lie. When I was a boy I denied my Jewishness to stay alive in Europe. Now, as a man, I have never really lived out my Christianity. I have run over people, lied, cheated, taken advantage of the poor -- all to build my financial empire. I don't know a single businessman in the world, Christian or not, who has not done the same thing. But my deepest sin is the way I neglected my wife, and my son. If I cannot hear her words from the grave, if I cannot hear truth, then what have I got to live for?"

"Listen to me, Simon. I know who you are. You are a sinner, of course, we all are. But you are a man of God, too. Don't wallow in the words of a sick woman."

Pedersen's eyes flashed as he slowly got to his feet, shoving the huge executive chair back against the credenza behind him. "Damn it, Bert," his words were strong, clipped, "I killed my wife. Don't be easy on me. Despite her drunkenness, she probably knew more about truth than you or I will ever know. Now read me the note!"

Jessup took a step backward. He had never seen Simon when he exerted raw authority. Bert quickly unfolded the note and continued, his voice shaking.

. . . Night after night I have lain awake in our bed, needing you, hating you. Even if you were home, you were always downstairs in that damned study of yours, dictating, talking on the phone, or, worst of all, playing Jesus games with your Christian friends. All the while you were running your empire from your brown leather throne, your family

*was dying around you. And you didn't care. Don't grieve
for me, Simon. I've been dead for years – only you haven't
noticed. If you want to inscribe anything on my tombstone,
it should be: "Died, at 33 -- buried 15 years later."*

*I make only one request, dear husband: for the sake of
the God you say you follow, help Mark. He's dying, too.
Are you so blinded by business that you cannot see it?
Please Simon, don't do to him what you've done to me.*

Jessup stopped reading and stood silently.
Simon was standing behind the desk, his rage
drained from him, his head down.

"She's right, you know," Pedersen finally said.

Jessup was struggling. "Simon, you know the
rules. Wait until the dust settles before you try to
pick up the pieces."

"Why don't you tell me the truth," Simon said
evenly, raising his head, his weight still supported
by his arms. He was looking straight into the
evangelist's eyes. "You know I killed my wife. I'm
killing my son. Why don't you just say so? Maybe
that way I can be forgiven."

Simon sat for a long time looking into the
blank, frozen face of Bert Jessup.

Jessup dropped his eyes. Eventually he spoke,
his voice quivering. "Simon, you know I can't tell
you that."

Pedersen nodded slowly, straightening up and
turning to the window -- his back toward Jessup. "I
know," he said softly. "And I know why. But that's
all right, Bert. Somehow I'll come through this --
even if I have to do it alone."

"That's the Silver Fisherman speaking," Bert
said, smiling in relief. "You've got long bootstraps.
Just reach for them and God will give you the

strength to pull yourself up."

Simon glanced at his watch. It was time to go. There was still no word from Mark. He had called the night before and talked to Simon's secretary, saying he would arrive in time for the funeral.

"Mark will show up as soon as he can," Bert said, walking around and putting a hand on Simon's shoulder. "Right now there are a hundred people out at the cemetery who love you, who have come from all over the world to pay their respect to Cynthia who died in a tragic accident."

"You know Mark hates me, don't you? My own son hates me." Simon's voice broke, and he reached up and grasped the hand of his old friend.

"Mark will come through this just as you will come through it," Bert said gently.

"I've got to make it up to him."

"You will."

"I've never given him anything but money: not my time, not myself. I've not even been able to talk to him about God. He's too bitter."

"Don't think about it now."

"He's like a man possessed by demons. Whenever he's around he glares at me."

"There's nothing any of us can do about that. He'll have to find his own bootstraps."

"God, it seems so hopeless."

"It's not hopeless. It's just the dark before the dawn."

"We're ready, Mr. Pedersen, Reverend Jessup." It was Simon's chauffeur, standing at the door of the study. "Mark called. He said he would meet you at the cemetery."

"You see," Bert said as the two men walked through the front door into the brilliant morning sunlight, "I told you God would work everything out. It's tomorrow that counts -- not today, and certainly not yesterday."

Although his father saved a chair for him under the canopy facing the closed casket, Mark had still not arrived when the service began. His car pulled up during the Scripture reading and he took his place near the back of the mourners who were standing around the grave. He had flown in from Lake Tahoe early that morning on a commercial airliner, having refused the company's offer to send a private plane. His dad saw him just as Jessup, standing at the head of the grave, finished his closing prayer. Simon quickly rose from the small folding chair where he was seated with a group of close family friends and started toward his son.

Mark was at the rear of the crowd near a giant maple tree. He was easy to spot, standing almost seven feet tall, his black hair tousled by the wind, his square chin jutted arrogantly. How much he looks like his Grandfather Jacoby, Simon thought, remembering vaguely his own father who had so bravely challenged the Nazis that night in Munich when they broke the windows of his bakery. He, too, had been a giant of a man, but he was no match for the Nazis who jailed and later executed him. Mark had those same stubborn features: those black eyes, the square, jutting chin.

He was dressed casually in an open-necked shirt and tweed sport jacket. He could have been a professional basketball player had he not been so spoiled. Even so, he was brilliant, the kind of man who not only stood out in a crowd because of his size but because of his poise. He had refused to let a Pedersen car meet him at the airport. Instead, he had arranged for one of his friends to pick him up and drive him directly to the cemetery.

Simon moved rapidly toward him, arms out to embrace his son. He was unprepared for Mark's angry reaction.

"It's a bit late for hugs, isn't it, *Father?*" Mark spit out as his dad reached for him.

Simon didn't hesitate. He moved right in. "Mark, I loved your mother more than you'll ever know. If you and I ever needed each other...."

Mark, turned to one side, threw his cigarette to the ground and crushed it into the soft green grass of the cemetery with the ball of his foot. He ignored his father's outstretched arms. His face was hard as he stepped to one side.

"Don't come around Mother's grave with that pious slop -- pretending you love me, pretending you loved her. You don't love anyone but yourself .You hurt her enough when she was alive. Don't dishonor her memory by dumping your lying garbage on me in front of all your friends."

The people around Mark had backed away. Embarrassed. They left the two men, the anguished businessman and his angry giant of a son, alone -- facing one another. Simon looked up into his son's eyes, blazing behind the thick, black-framed glasses. God, how much he looked like his own father had looked.

"Look at you," Mark scoffed. "Your black and silver clothes. Your pockets full of money. It meant nothing to her -- it means nothing to me."

Bert Jessup moved between the two men. He laid a hand on Simon's arm. "He has a right to his feelings, Simon. Let's go home and give him a chance to cool off. Then you can talk."

Simon pulled away, his face ashen as he looked up at his angry son. "Please, Mark. I admit I've been a failure. I failed your mother. I've failed you. But I am prepared to go anywhere to make it up to you."

"Then go to hell, Father!" Mark sneered.

He turned and stalked back to his friend's car.

For almost a week Simon continued in his depression. He demanded to be left alone. The curtains drawn and the telephone unplugged, he dismissed all his domestic servants except the security police at the gate. The only one he might have been willing to talk to was Bert Jessup, but the evangelist had to return to Florida for the next taping of his Jesus World TV program. Simon was not disappointed. He preferred to be alone with his grief.

Simon was right about the autopsy. It revealed Cynthia had taken a lethal dose of amphetamines. Suicide is the ultimate insult, he realized, the ultimate rejection. It was his helpless wife's only way of getting his attention, of saying to him: "You failed me. I needed you and you were never around to help me." A man can be a success in all his business ventures, he can own hundreds of hotels and thousands of newspapers, by one sale he can shake the entire stock market, he can be written up in *Forbes, Business Week* and *Barrens,* he can serve on the board of directors for the Trilateral Commission -- but if he fails in the most intimate of all relations, with his wife and son, he is a failure.

A lesser man, a man who did not feel deeply, a man with shallow sensitivity, could have shrugged it off. He could have poured himself back into his business. He could have agreed with Jessup's philosophy and lived for tomorrow. But somehow

Simon sensed that he had to deal with his yesterdays before he could move on to tomorrow. He remembered his last conversation with Cynthia before he left to meet Bert Jessup in Florida She had been drinking. He warned her to quit or he would have to send her off to the hospital again.

"Simon, I don't need a hospital. I just need you."

He remembered how frightened that made him feel. He knew she was trying to drag him into her world of confused feelings. To have entered would have meant he would have to spend great lengths of time, time which he felt could be far better spent in productive matters. So he had quickly kissed her on the cheek and promised her, as he had promised her countless times before, that he would be back and they would talk about it then.

But when he closed the door on her, she knew - - as he would have known if he had not been so busy -- that "then" would never come.

Sitting in the darkened formal dining room, the great velvet curtains drawn and a half-emptied bottle of expensive Scotch sitting before him, he re-lived that terrible scene on the Danish fishing trawler when he was 11 years old. The Danish sailors were kind. They had smuggled him and his mother out of Copenhagen in the early morning hours. For two hours he and his mother had lain silently under a smelly canvas tarp on the deck as the fishermen piled their traps around them. They sailed just before dawn, going out with all the other boats. Once at sea, the sailors had pulled back the tarp and kidded with him. He had a smudge of tar under his nose, and they called him Little Hitler. To compensate, he had acted brave, pretended he wasn't afraid.

Then came the evening and the sounds of the approaching German patrol boat. The Germans had no official authority over the Danes at that time, for the war had not yet begun. But everyone knew the Germans were killing Jews wherever they could find them. And reports had filtered back of the Germans stopping Danish and Dutch boats, searching them, and shooting Jews on deck and throwing their bodies into the sea. Quickly the sailors hid the mother and son in the galley cupboards -- his mother on one side of the tiny kitchen, and Simon, because he was so small, crouched in a cabinet beneath the sink, his head wedged between the pipes.

He could barely breathe. When he heard the German patrol boat bounce off the side of the fishing trawler, he messed his pants. It was the most humiliating thing that had ever happened to him. But he could not move -- only squat there with his head wedged between the pipes, shaking and crying.

When the all-clear signal was given and the mate rapped on the cupboard laughing and telling "Little Hitler" he could come out, that his cousins had gone back to Germany, he refused to leave his dark, cramped, smelly quarters. He would rather stay in the cupboard, wallowing in his own mess, than face the light and let the sailors know who he really was -- a little Jewish boy who couldn't control his bowels.

But they had pulled him out. And, as he feared, laughed at him for using the galley as a head. He was mortified. Humiliated. He tried to act brave, but his stained trousers spoke louder than all his words. He broke, ran to the deck and tried to jump overboard. Only the strong arm of a

young sailor saved him. His mother rinsed out his
trousers, but he spent the rest of the trip below
deck, sitting sullenly in the corner of a cabin.

Simon Pedersen poured himself another drink.
He had tried to pray -- but could he approach a holy
God with the blood of his wife on his hands? And
his failure as a father. There was no deck to dash
for, no sea to throw himself into. Not here in
Wayne, Illinois. He gulped down the drink and
headed for his study. In the top right hand drawer
was the only weapon he had ever owned -- a pearl-
handled Luger his stepfather had taken from the
body of a German soldier in Norway. That was the
best way out. Maybe, in the next life, he could make
it up to Cynthia.

IV

SIMON STOOD AT THE DOOR of the study, his fingers resting on the decorated bronze doorknob. Cynthia had picked out the hardware for the house when they had it built five years before. It was she who insisted his study be located at the foot of the stairs, just off the front door. "Your business always comes first," she had said with a hint of sarcasm in her voice. "A man who never comes home from work without his brief case should greet his study the first thing when he walks in the house. He can always find time to kiss his wife later."

They joked about it afterwards. But the door of the study, just feet from where his wife's stiffening body had been found the week before, suddenly loomed like the entrance to a tomb. He twisted the knob to enter. The gun was waiting.

But he never stepped into the room. The chiming of the doorbell interrupted him. Who? He had given specific instructions to the security guards to admit no one. Only his chauffeur, who lived in the carriage house at the rear of the property, had the privilege of entering. And he only through the service entrance at the back. And only after calling ahead of time. But this was the front doorbell.

Pedersen turned and stared at the closed door, then walked mechanically, like a robot, to open the door.

Simon blinked at the bright day. It had been five days since he had been outside the house.

The early afternoon sun was bathing the front lawn, casting shadows from the trees near the front gate. Birds were chirping around the fountain in the circular driveway. Far away he heard the roar of a jet taking off from an airport -- perhaps from the private strip at Pedersen Enterprises. He stood blinking in the light, his face unshaved, his silver hair which was nearly always combed in a modified pompadour hanging in straggles over his ears.

Squinting his eyes, he focused on the man standing in the door. He was short, stocky, with dark skin and coal black hair. Indian. He looked like an Indian. He was dressed in a country western suit with cowboy boots. He had a felt cowboy hat in his hand. His black eyes twinkled as he extended his hand.

"Mr. Pedersen, I'm not sure you remember me. I'm Joe Panther from Koinonia Ranch. God told me to come see you."

Consumed with loneliness, confused with grief and guilt, Simon Pedersen opened the door and said, "If ever a man needed a visit from God, it's me. Come in."

Despite the fact Joe Panther came from another world -- culturally and racially -- Simon Pedersen realized he was indeed a man sent from God. For five hours they sat in Simon's study, talking.

"I waited three days after hearing of your wife's death," the muscular man said "Then, day before yesterday, after I came in from mending fences on the ranch, I felt God was telling me it was time to come see you. I rode the bus all yesterday and last night, arriving in Chicago this morning."

"How did you get past the security guards at the gate?" Simon asked.

Panther grinned shyly. "The taxi let me off in front of the house. I prayed and just walked through the gate. It's not unheard of, you know, for God to blind the eyes of the opposition."

As Joe Panther talked, Simon could understand why Walt Disney had been fascinated by this man. The son of a Seminole Indian chief who had married a white schoolteacher, Panther had grown up in the little Florida town of Immokalee. His father was a rancher but Joe turned down several offers to ride the rodeo circuit in order to go to college and seminary. He held a doctor's degree in New Testament Greek and after teaching for a while almost went into fulltime evangelism. Despite his popularity on the preaching circuit, however, he never could shake the call to return to the ranch. He finally gave up his public ministry and went home to spend time with the cowboys in central Florida. At first he spent his time preaching at cattle auctions and riding the range with his Bible. Eventually he established Koinonia Ranch – a combination training school for cowboys and a rehabilitation center for alcoholics. It was during this time that Walt Disney, who was then building his fabulous Disney World, urged Pedersen to provide land for Panther to build his center.

There was something about this man -- strong, quiet, intellectually brilliant, yet unassuming -- that appealed to the deepest instincts of Simon Pedersen. To some degree he reminded him of his stepfather, with his calloused hands and little laugh-lines around his eyes.

When Simon began to weep quietly, saying he was responsible for his wife's death, Panther listened, but he did not try to pacify. He agreed that despite Simon's devotion to God, he had sinned against his wife – and against his son.

"Then there is no way out. Cynthia is dead. What hope do I have?" He couldn't keep his eyes from drifting to the top right hand drawer of his desk where the Luger was hidden.

Slowly Joe Panther explained the process of forgiveness. "It starts with recognition of sin. That is followed by confession and repentance. Only then does God forgive.

"What you have done has been wrong," Panther said "Your wife might be here today had you put her first in your life -- rather than your business, or your ministry. But if God forgave Paul, who was responsible for the death of Stephen, if he forgave Simon Peter, who was responsible -- in a real measure -- for the death of Jesus, will He not forgive Simon Pedersen?"

They prayed together, two men alone in the darkened mansion, and for the first time since Cynthia died, Simon felt release. Joe Panther was not an intruder into his grief, he was the way out. By the time the evening shadows grew long on the manicured lawn and the red leaves of the ornamental Japanese maples had turned to deep gray with the setting of the sun, Simon Pedersen, the Silver Fisherman, had been set free.

Joe Panther did not stay, despite Pedersen's plea for him to spend the night. He made a few suggestions as to how Simon should approach his son. He would not even accept Simon's pressed offer for him to fly home in a Pedersen jet, agreeing only to have the chauffeur drive him back to the bus station.

"I came to deliver a message," Panther said kindly. "I do not want to confuse that with financial reward -- at least not at this time. Perhaps one day you will want to come to Koinonia Ranch and let Jesus make you more than a captain on a yacht. He will make you a real fisher of men. The decision must be yours, however."

He picked up his cowboy hat and started to leave. Pedersen reached for him, embracing him. It was first time in his adult life he had embraced a man. He felt the tears coming once again as Joe Panther's strong arms encircled him, drawing him close to his muscular chest.

Panther smiled, stepped back, and disappeared through the door.

Pedersen returned to his paneled study and stood for a long moment in the center of the room. Although the house was now in total darkness, he was no longer alone. He sensed a presence. Was it the Holy Spirit? He moved from room to room in the darkness, trying desperately to remember Cynthia. Odd, but the tears simply would not flow. Instead he wanted to sing. Old songs from childhood flooded his mind. Then in the darkness he was singing out loud -- in Norwegian. It was like drinking from a spring after days of thirsting in the desert.

The cleansing from guilt, from sin, from selfishness -- the thing he had tried to do all those years by working so hard for God -- it was complete. He had never felt such exhilaration. The words and music flowed from his lips. It was as if a spring, long clogged with debris, had suddenly been raked clear. The singing lasted almost an hour, and even after it died down the exhilaration, the feeling of release from guilt, the feeling of forgiveness, remained.

Simon turned on the light in the big kitchen and moved toward the refrigerator. He had not eaten in three days. It was time to begin living.

Early the next morning Simon called Mark, who was staying downtown in the executive suite of the Chicago Pedersen.

"Can I see you sometime today, son?" he asked

"I have nothing to say to you."

"But I have something important to say to you, Mark, or do you want to sever all connection with Pedersen Enterprises?"

There was a long silence. "I'll come to your office this afternoon. 3 p.m. okay?"

"That's fine."

Simon hung up with a sigh of relief. The first small bridge had been crossed in the rebuilding of the relationship. He hated to use leverage to arrange a meeting with his son, but knew he might never see Mark again if he didn't. A different approach had to be used than at the gravesite.

Mark arrived at Simon's office forty minutes late, with an insolent look on his face. He sprawled in one of the soft chairs, lit a cigarette and began flicking ashes on the rug. "Are you going to fire me, Father?" he drawled.

"I'm sorry I embarrassed you at Cynthia's grave," Simon began evenly. "I was in a state of shock and remorse. I wanted affection from you which you weren't able to give. I was wrong to seek it."

Mark grunted.

"I don't think I know what it means to be a father, but I'd like to learn."

"Try it with someone else, please."

"Then you want nothing more to do with me?"

"That's right."

"Nor with the company?"

"Must one go with the other?"

Simon was silent a moment, running his finger along the side of his desk. "No. You can work for the company, but it may be hard to avoid me unless you take a low-level job."

"I'd like that."

"A low-level job?"

"Yes."

"Where?"

"As far from you as possible."

"Let's see. We have a hotel in Thailand. Would you like to go there as manager?"

"As assistant manager."

"Okay, Mark, I'll arrange it"

"Is that all you want of me?" Mark stared hard at his father.

"That's all"

Mark pulled his gangling body upright, walked to the door, hesitated, then turned around. One question: why did you sic the Indian on me?"

"The Indian? What do you mean?" Simon's surprise was total.

"This Joe Panther. He called me this noon from a bus station. Preached God at me over the phone. I figured you put him up to it and told him to get lost"

"Joe Panther saved my life yesterday. Maybe he was trying to save yours as well, Mark."

"What does that mean?"

Simon sighed "It's a long story, son. I hope I'll have a chance to tell you sometime. I'm going down to his ranch in a few days and try to learn how to be a human being again."

"What kind of ranch does he have?"

Simon spent five minutes telling all he knew about Joe Panther, grateful for the extra dialogue with his son. Mark did show interest in the ranch's physical program, but his eyes began to cloud up when Simon described the religious emphasis.

"Tell Panther I'm not interested, will you Dad?" Mark turned to go out the door.

"One more thing, son." Simon cleared his throat as Mark turned around "Regardless of how you feel toward me, I love you."

For a fraction of a moment Mark's guard came down. He blinked, swallowed, then nodded awkwardly and left.

Simon stared for a long moment at the door through which his son had walked. Then he called in his secretary and dictated a quick memo to his chief executive officer. "My son, Mark, would like to start as an assistant manager of one of our hotels. Give him a choice of two. The one in Thailand or the one in Atlanta."

Then he called Bert Jessup. "You have been patient, good friend, during my time of agony. I think the Lord has been speaking to us both. Go ahead with your big plans for Jesus World and I'll instruct my lawyers to draw up the necessary papers."

"That's marvelous news, Simon. What about you? I need you in this too."

"That must come later, Bert. Right now I have some repair work to do -- on both the inner and outer man."

Not until late the next day did he reach Joe Panther. "I'm ready to pick up that option you said would be waiting," Simon said. "Can you teach me all you know about God if I come down there for a few weeks?"

"I can teach you how to string a barbed wire fence in two days -- that is, if you don't get snake bit I can teach you how to drain a septic tank in one afternoon. But to learn about God will take you the rest of your life -- and maybe more."

"Well, I'd better get started then," Pedersen said, a catch in his voice. "I'll arrive in Orlando tomorrow at 4 p.m. Can you meet my plane?"

IT WAS STRANGE, stepping onto property he had owned for years but never seen. Simon Pedersen had studied the report handed him by his vice president in charge of real estate, but it contained almost no information on Joe Panther's operation at Koinonia Ranch.

Simon discovered that Panther had never taken anything from him except the free lease. All the buildings had been built with volunteer labor, with donations from Christians around the state. The two-story lodge, for instance, which was the central building doubling as a chapel, dining hall, and dormitory, had been built by a building contractor who spent a year at Koinonia Ranch recovering from alcoholism.

Joe Panther parked his battered pickup truck outside the concrete block lodge. Turning off the ignition, he looked over at Simon.

"We're all the same here," he said. "Cowboy and corporation president. We all sweat. We all work. We all pray. And we do it together."

They got out of the truck and Panther helped unload the suitcases from the back. He grinned as Simon brushed straw and dust off his leather bag. Looking down at Pedersen's expensive shoes, Panther said, "How long has it been since you got cow manure on those alligator slippers?"

"Don't tell me that's part of becoming a disciple too?" Simon said, wrinkling his brow.

"Jesus started in a stable," Panther said. "Are you better than Him?"

Pedersen took a deep breath. "I guess I have a lot to learn about the Kingdom of God, don't I?"

"The Kingdom does not have its headquarters on Wall Street -- or even in Chicago. Neither is it pews and altars. It's people. Real people. People who hurt. People who cry at night. People who swear. People who laugh. People who love. Tomorrow we'll go into town and buy you some jeans, boots, and gloves. Those soft hands will need help when you start pulling barbed wire. But that's where we start becoming a man of God around here. In the field."

Inside the lodge, Panther took Pedersen up the stairs to his room at the end of the hall. It was comfortable but rustic. The windows were open with screens to keep out the flying insects. There was no air conditioning, but a ceiling fan whirred steadily, moving the air gradually around the room which was paneled with rough cypress. There was a double bed, a single dresser, a small desk, and a closet.

"The bath is next door. The other fellows share it with you, so keep track of your stuff. Some of the men haven't quite gotten used to the eighth commandment yet."

"Eighth commandment?"

Panther chuckled "You do have a long way to go, don't you? You know, 'Thou shalt not steal.'"

Pedersen looked down at his soft hands with the manicured nails. It had been a long time since he pulled fish traps with his stepfather off the coast of Norway. Now his physical activity was confined to tennis every Saturday morning and perhaps a swim at the club. No wonder Mark had accused him of being plastic. Now he would become real. There would be dirt under his fingernails, scratches on his arms, and calluses on his hands. Not only that, but he was living among thieves. It scared him, but the thrill of adventure, the determination to overcome, the same drive that had put him on top of one of the nation's largest corporations, was now stirring in his gut, and the call from the mountain was clearer than it had ever been before.

"I'm ready," Pedersen said, looking into Panther's dark eyes. "Just don't leave me alone."

"I'll be right beside you," Joe said as they came down the stairs into the noisy dining room, filled with men in work clothes eating from metal trays at the tables.

Koinonia Ranch was a simple operation. Besides the lodge and a smaller dorm used to house permanent staff, there were several small houses and trailers around the area. The latter were for those with families who brought their wives and children. All in all, there were about 20 people on the ranch -- six of whom were on staff.

Most of the men in the training program were young. Rodeo riders, ranch hands, construction workers. A few had been on drugs or alcohol. Two were on leave of absence from a nearby prison. Only one other man came from the business world like Pedersen. He was the attorney general from a northern state who had been convicted of fraud and malfeasance of office. The judge, who knew of Panther's work, had paroled him to Koinonia Ranch for a year.

Panther's program was regimented but with meaning. Long ago Joe had rejected the institutional pattern that the way to disciple Christians was to bring them into a church service once a week. Real disciples, he believed, had to catch the spirit of the disciple maker. That meant living together.

"Men learn on three levels," he told the group the next morning as they gathered for Bible study after breakfast in the dining hall. "Most churches teach by dispensing information. They scatter Bible facts like seeds dropped from an airplane over a city. Most of it falls on concrete. A few seeds may fall in the cracks of sidewalks, but it doesn't take long before they are crushed. The only ones that take root are those that fall in the gutters. They may grow and bloom, but the first heavy rain washes them away too.

"There is a second level on which we learn. It is called 'formational' learning. We do a lot of that around here. This is the forming and shaping of lives by example and personal contact. Some of you have never learned to love your wife, much less another man. You'll learn that by watching us as we live together. The same is true of picking tomatoes or pruning fruit trees. We learn by doing.

"But the highest form of teaching was the kind used by Jesus: teaching by revelation. Jesus wanted to bring His disciples to the place where He could say to them, as He said to Peter, 'Blessed art thou, Simon son of Jonah: for flesh and blood hath not revealed it unto thee, but my Father which is in heaven.' Jesus wants us to come to the place where we hear from the Father as frequently and accurately as He did.

"Most church leaders spend their time building institutions. Out here we are building men. I am no longer going to spread my seed on concrete. I want mine to take root, not in a gutter, but in a field where it produces fruit; for in the center of each fruit are a hundred new seeds."

Simon looked around at the group of men, most of whom had weathered faces. All were nodding their heads. They were as serious as their leader when it came to the Kingdom of God.

Joe loved the small group setting. Seated in a circle around the room each morning after breakfast, the men not only listened intently but were encouraged to challenge him on every point. And while the Bible was the center of his teaching, he roamed into all the fields of literature, the arts, the sciences. But it was outside, when the men worked on the ranch and in the fields, that the real teaching took place.

"It is not enough to teach a man how to read a compass, or even how to take it apart and fix it when it goes wrong. He needs to know how to walk north."

It took Simon less than a week before he realized he needed to stay longer. His hands were blistered, his face sunburned, his legs sore from walking in the unaccustomed cowboy boots – but he was loving it. He was also feeling much better about Mark. He had called his son and, while the conversation was a bit strained, there was communication. Mark had decided to take the job with the Atlanta Pedersen hotel.

I'm not sure how long I'm supposed to stay here," Simon told Joe Panther one evening after supper. "But I'm ready to stay as long as necessary."

Panther grinned "I figured you'd say that after you had been here awhile. I'll work you into the regular rotation shift so you can get a taste of everything we're doing."

"I promised Bert Jessup I would spend time with him too," Simon said. "It won't be long before they are breaking ground for his Jesus World."

"I've heard about it," Joe replied. "I just hope they won't be running their machines across our pastures."

"Jessup promised me, when we transferred the property, that he would not touch this back acreage."

Panther nodded slowly. "God is still in control, even if I don't understand it all."

Simon started his regular job rotation in the slaughter-house. Later he tried his hand at cutting meat, working in the feed lot, riding herd, mending fences, and planting crops.

Joe worked with each group. He believed the best way to teach a man theology was to show him how to set fence posts, plant a straight row, or brand a cow. "There's nothing that will bring out the old nature like picking okra in the broiling sun," he chuckled. "I've a problem with my temper. When it blows I know it's time for me to get my hands in the earth."

Simon's first assignment in the feed lot was to dig a ditch to carry off the waste from the cows. For the first time since he had been at the ranch, he resisted and complained to Panther.

Pushing his hat back and mopping his brow with a red bandana, the muscular Indian lashed back at Simon. "How a man digs a ditch is indicative of his character," he said with eyes flashing. "If he digs it according to specification he's learned obedience. If he trims the sides, squares out the bottom, cuts all the roots and piles the excess dirt neatly so it can be returned to the ditch, I know I can trust him in other matters as well. If he gripes and complains, it makes me wonder about his spiritual maturity.

"If you're here for a vacation, or to prove something to your dead wife, or to play the role of a man for your son, it would be better if you left now."

Simon stared at the angry Indian in amazement. It was the first time, since he was a boy, he had been so sharply rebuked. Somehow, it seemed justified. Maybe he was learning something after all.

God, it turned out, was not at all as he imagined. He had always thought of Him as one of those marble statues, hard and cold-removed from life. Now he saw Him in the smiling faces of the rough men at the dinner table. He heard Him rustle in the palm leaves as he sat at his dawn devotions on a rough log near the cattle pen. He heard Him in the laughter of the little children playing around the ranch. And once he thought he even saw Jesus working side by side with him as he grunted and sweated with four other men, slinging hay with pitchforks from a trailer into the barn.

As he met God, he also discovered himself. He had long forgotten who the real Simon Pedersen was. The reality of life he had experienced as a child had been replaced with the artificiality of the corporate image. Instead of a man who laughed, loved, and cried, he had become a machine dressed in a three-piece suit, wearing a gold wristwatch and carrying a genuine leather attaché case with a combination lock. His hair was razor cut weekly in a stylish salon on the 17th floor of a building he owned in downtown Chicago. He seldom drove his own car, but sat in the back seat of a chauffeur-driven limousine with a private telephone and a computer terminal. He rang bells, pushed buttons, and people appeared and disappeared.

Perhaps the real Simon Pedersen was reappearing, dressed in faded jeans and boots. His silver hair, which had turned to a craggy mane, was tucked under a sweat-stained cowboy hat. His hands were calloused and his face bronzed. He was coming alive. When he swung a grubbing hoe to dig out palmetto stumps, he felt energy surging through his body. When he sat on the tailgate of Joe Panther's pickup truck, climbed into the rusted metal seat of the old farm tractor, or put shoulder to the rump of a stubborn cow and shoved her into a stall, he knew he was in the mainstream of life.

For the first time in his life Simon was not giving orders. Instead, he was learning the spiritual principle that until a man submits, he has no real authority. He submitted to Joe Panther, who told him to learn from a young Indian boy with long hair who had never learned to read but knew how to butcher a cow and cut the meat into steaks and roasts faster than any man he had ever seen. He submitted to a former deputy sheriff who had recently been released from prison after taking part in a drug smuggling operation. From him he learned how to saddle a horse, de-horn a mean cow, castrate young bulls, and even throw a rope around a bucking calf. By these men of low estate, who were teaching him about life, he was called things like stupid, incompetent, and thick-headed.

He loved it -- even Panther's occasional temper outbursts. He felt healthier, happier, and more of a man than ever in his life.

Each Monday morning Simon was on the phone with his son. They started out discussing business matters. Mark seemed to be enjoying his new responsibilities in the Atlanta hotel, although there was still some evidence he had not deserted his playboy life. But as the weeks and months went by, Simon found himself using the Monday morning phone conversations to talk to Mark about what he was learning from Joe Panther. Gradually Mark seemed to be listening.

"Don't get your hopes too high," Panther warned him one afternoon, as the two men rode their horses through the high grass looking for stray calves. "If a man comes to God as a child, it's always easier. Once the world has a grip on him, however, it takes a lot of breaking -- and pain -- before a man can make a serious commitment."

They were interrupted by the sound of heavy earth-moving equipment rumbling by. The sounds of the machinery at Jesus World next door were becoming louder and louder.

VI

THE BEST MINDS in America had gone to work designing Jesus World. Architects, engineers, landscapers, physicists. No expenses were spared. Biblical archeologists and Bible scholars had been hired to draw up the plans. Jessup retained a management consulting firm to raise the money, and millions of dollars had been pouring in.

In the first six months, Jessup's team finished a full-scale, three-dimensional, electronically operated mock-up -- the size of a basketball court. Construction crews were at the same time breaking ground. Buildings were soaring skyward.

Simon Pedersen soon found himself spending every weekend with Jessup rather than going out with the witnessing teams from Koinonia Ranch into prisons and mental institutions. One day Simon announced that he felt it was time for him to leave the ranch. Panther did not resist. Except for two visits to Atlanta to see Mark, Simon had stayed ten months at the ranch, longer than he originally planned.

The grand opening for Jesus World was scheduled for the week before Christmas, when Florida would be teeming with tourists. It was to be, without question, a spectacular event. And if there was one thing Bert Jessup had learned from his experience on TV, it was that you had to entertain the viewer if you wanted to keep him.

"That's what's wrong with today's churches," he pointed out to Pedersen. "Not enough flair. When church attendance goes down and the money falls off, it's because they're too stodgy and dull. A hundred years ago the local church had no competition. It was the social center, the political forum, the town hall, the farmers' grange, the place for the Saturday afternoon picnic and the women's quilting bee. Now the church has to compete with bowling alleys, professional football, disco houses, skating rinks, not to mention Disney World and TV. It's no wonder the church is falling behind -- it's still living in another century. You can't attract today's young person or the wealthy businessman with stale sermons and dead liturgy. Today you have to command people's attention. At Jesus World we're going to major on good, solid family entertainment -- but give the people the gospel at the same time."

Everyone Jessup talked to was enthusiastic. His advisory board included two Methodist bishops, a Catholic cardinal, the rector of America's largest Episcopal church, a representative from Full Gospel Business Men's Fellowship, two nationwide evangelists, a famous Pentecostal faith healer, the president of a Presbyterian seminary, the dean of the largest rabbinical school in the nation, several outstanding Christian financiers, and the president of the Southern Baptist Convention.

"What Mecca is to the Moslems, the Mormon Tabernacle is to the Latter Day Saints, and Jerusalem is to the Jews -- so will Jesus World be to all Christians," Jessup pronounced. The plan was similar to Walt Disney World. There would be a number of "attractions," all depicting Biblical scenes. A sophisticated plan for moving people through the park had been designed by the nation's finest engineers and architects. Two giant Pedersen Hotels were under construction just outside the gate.

At first Jessup wanted to limit the attractions to scenes from the New Testament. He had in mind experiences for every one -- of the Disney variety -- complete with a scale model of the Herodian Temple, boat rides down the Jordan River, holograms of Jesus walking on the water, and the old Jerusalem marketplace where tourists could browse in quaint shops along the winding streets and purchase souvenirs. However, the Jewish member of the board quickly convinced him that there should be an entire section of the park devoted to Old Testament scenes -- beginning with the Creation and including Noah's Ark for children.

As the work on the park progressed, Jessup seemed to come up with a new idea every day -- sometimes two a day. What had started out to be a replica of some Bible scenes using wax figures was quickly growing into something so big that even Simon, with all his imagination, had not been able to conceive. Simon knew the danger of too rapid growth at the beginning of a project, and he tried to warn Jessup. But the evangelist was working as a man possessed, saying it was God who woke him in the middle of the night with vivid descriptions of how to build the next project.

One afternoon Simon confronted Bert in the construction office. He had just been out to the park site and found earth-movers piling up dirt for a huge attraction called the Mt. Sinai

Rollercoaster.

"Bert, we've got to stick to the original plans. These other attractions can be added later. But if you're not careful, you'll spend all your investor's money before the park even opens."

"Simon, you've no idea how much money has been pouring in from all over the world People are sick of all this secular humanism. They're ready for something wholesome, something Biblical. And they're backing it up with their money. Last week we received 18 million dollars in investments – and more is coming in this week."

"But all that has to be paid back one of these days," Simon warned.

"God woke me up last night," Bert said seriously. "Not only did He give me the exact blueprint for the Mt. Sinai Rollercoaster, but He told me we would break into the black inside of two years. I have no choice but to follow God. If I deviate with even one project, He might withdraw His blessing."

Simon looked closely at Jessup. The likeable evangelist was ever one brimming with creative ideas -- always a man of action. To Simon he now seemed too wound up, like an overheated, out-of-sync racing engine on a fast car. Simon had had sad experience with executives like this before.

"Slow it down, Bert. You're trying to do too much too soon."

"We can't slow down now," Jessup said enthusiastically, rising to his feet and pacing the floor. "Look at this."

He threw copies of *Newsweek* and *Time* across the desk so Simon could see the covers. Jessup's face was on the cover of both magazines. *Time* called him "God's Entrepreneur."

"This will be the Taj Mahal, Sistine Chapel, Westminster Abbey, the Holy Land, and Ringling Brothers Circus all combined," he intoned. "By the time we finish, we'll be bigger than Walt Disney World, Circus World, and Sea World all together."

"I'd still feel a lot more comfortable if you had a group of wise Christians around you as counselors," Simon replied.

"I have my advisory board. It's made up of the finest religious minds in the world."

"And you meet with them every other month for six hours."

Bert Jessup sighed, mopped his forehead and sat down again in his chair. "Okay, Simon. I hear you. I do move too fast I need you to keep me on the right track at the right speed."

"That's better," Simon said relieved. "We can't let this thing turn into some kind of Frankenstein monster that devours us all."

On several occasions during the time Jesus World was under construction, Simon had met with Joe Panther to discuss the project. "There are many ministries in the Kingdom of God," Panther told him one afternoon as the two men sat on the front porch of the lodge at Koinonia Ranch. "I'm grateful for men like Billy Graham -- but I am not called to mass evangelism. I am called to supplement what he is doing, make a few disciples and send them back into the world."

"Why then can't you get enthused about Jesus World?"

"I used to listen to Jessup's TV program, and I enjoyed it. He has brought people to Jesus Christ and I honor him for that. I don't know, Simon -- I guess I resist the big approach to soul saving which always seems to need a lot of money."

"Nearly all the local pastors are enthusiastic," Simon said.

Pedersen grinned back. "Compromises seem to be necessary in every part of life -- even Christian work."

Panther shook his head "If I bought that I'd leave the Christian faith for something else."

"You've been fortunate, Joe. You haven't had to scrounge for money to pay your bills. No one has pushed you for an account of how many souls you've saved. You've been left alone to do your thing."

"That's true, Simon."

"Bert may not need your support, Joe, but I do. That's why I want you to come over to Jesus World and give us your counsel."

"Okay, Simon, I'll come over and take a look. But something tells me the day will come when I'll wish I had just stayed home in my swamp and been shepherd to my little flock."

The basic planning for Jesus World was being done in the Pedersen Triple Towers Hotel, which was located, ironically, just outside the gates of Walt Disney World. Simon had arranged for Jessup to take over the entire third and fourth floors of the hotel. The three-dimensional mock-up for Jesus World was located there, as well as the financial offices and the planning rooms for the Bible scholars, all of whom were now on the staff.

Simon himself did not have an office. He chose to leave all the operations to Jessup. But when he moved from Koinonia Ranch, he took up residence in one of the penthouses in the Triple Towers where he could be close to the action. It was in this suite that he confronted Bert Jessup with the fact it was time to include Joe Panther.

Jessup objected. "This Indian friend of yours lives in a different world, Simon," he warned. "People like this always slow down the work. You have to stop and explain -- defend -- every concept, every method."

"That may not be as bad as it sounds," Pedersen said, sitting behind his desk in the penthouse living room. The huge plate glass windows behind him opened on the panorama of orange groves, lakes, and busy highway.

"We're still moving too fast," Simon continued. "A good fisherman knows he must keep his bow into the sea and maintain deliberate speed, or his boat will swamp. But if you go too fast, you'll outrun the fish."

"God gives different gifts to different people," Jessup said, his voice rising. "Panther is a cowboy evangelist. I've been called to build Jesus World. The two simply don't go together."

"Bert," Simon said easily, leaning back in his chair and watching the evangelist through laughing eyes, "did you know that when you get excited, you breathe out of your mouth and nostrils simultaneously? My wife had a dog like that when we were first married -- a Boston bull. He was a little brown dog with a nose that looked like it had been smashed into his face by running into a stone wall. When he was upset, he sniffed and snorted, just like you're doing now."

Jessup stood, leaning forward over Pedersen's desk, supporting his body on his hands. For a long moment he stared at the silver-haired man. Then he laughed and relaxed. "If you and I start disagreeing, we'll just make it easier for the devil to destroy this project. I'll meet with Panther -- and anyone else you suggest."

VII

JOE PANTHER ARRIVED at the front gate of
Jesus World on December 15, three days before
the grand opening. Although he had been aware
of some of the things going on, he could hardly
believe his eyes as he viewed the immensity of
the construction which had taken place in just a
year -- and less than two miles from his little
ranch.

"The vice president is flying down for the
grand opening," Simon told him as they looked
toward the huge bank of ticket offices. "There
will be delegations from every major
denomination, plus a special envoy from the
Vatican. The mayor of Jerusalem is coming as
our guest of honor to cut the ribbon on the gate
of the Temple."

Panther just shook his head in disbelief.
What had been a quiet cow pasture just a year
before, surrounding Bert Jessup's little Jesus
World Ministries headquarters building with its
three small gardens, was now covered with
pavement, buildings, hotels, and the largest
amusement park he had ever seen.

"Come on," Simon said. "Bert is waiting
inside. He's agreed to give you a personal tour."

The muscular rancher said nothing but
followed the two men across the tarmac to a
waiting Electro-mover, which would take them
first to the hotels and then inside the park itself.

Everyone else who had been through the

park had gasped in amazement. Some had shouted "Hallelujah!" Others had wept from the beauty and awesomeness of the Biblical scenes. Everyone, absolutely everyone -- from seminary president to the delegation of Catholic bishops, to the president of ITT, to the Secretary of Commerce -- had been impressed.

Joe Panther's cold black eyes took in *every* detail. He walked as his forefathers had walked through the Sea of Grass, the Everglades, with soft steps -- as though he expected a snake to dart from a bush and strike. He listened, examined, his face without expression.

"I'd hate to play poker with that man," Simon thought. "He could be holding a handful of junk and bluff me out of a full house with aces high." But the stakes here were much bigger than any poker game.

"We've been moving fast, Joe," Simon said as they approached the front of the 22-story Bethlehem Pedersen Hotel, which was already open and booking guests. "I'm sorry I haven't had a chance to show you all this before. But I really do want your opinion."

Panther turned and looked straight into the eyes of Simon Pedersen. "You can count on that," he said.

Simon knew Joe was not intimidated by him. But he wondered if Jessup was right. Maybe Panther had been out of circulation too long. Maybe he didn't realize the potential of this project. After all, people would be coming from all over the world to attend Jesus World. Many of them would ask about Joe's Cowboy Chapel. Many would give money. If Joe was willing to cooperate with Pedersen and Jessup, it could be

the biggest thing ever to happen to Koinonia
Ranch. It, too, would grow.

Pedersen knew, too, that Panther was not
impressed with bigness. He could have been a
Christian celebrity if he had wished, but he had
turned his back on fame and fanfare to return to the
ranches of Central Florida and live his life among
the cowboys. That, among other things, was what
had attracted Pedersen to the somber-faced man
who was part Indian, part cowboy. Now he felt an
inner need for Panther's approval of Jesus World.

Taking their cue from near-by Walt Disney
World, the planners had gone far beyond the
imagination of that early Magic Kingdom visionary.
The park was surrounded by a facsimile of the walls
of the old City of Jerusalem. Stones from Israel had
been imported and were on the property. In the
middle, like Disney's Cinderella castle, stood an
exact scale reproduction of Herod's Temple, which
was standing at the time of Jesus -- complete with
escalators, moving sidewalks, and lifelike robots
who actually acted out the biblical events.

Simon had opposed the robots, urging Jessup to
stick with the original idea of using wax figures.
However, Bert had hired a brilliant young
electronics expert as his chief engineer. It was this
man who came in from the technical world. A
native Israeli by the name of Yosef Ben-Korach,
who had convinced him the robots were the key to
Jesus World. They would be controlled by
individual computers, the programs of which could
all be developed by Pedersen's giant computer
house in Belgium.

Inside the walls of the city were a number of
biblical attractions called A Walk Through the

Bible. These, too, were manned by robots.

Pausing on the beautiful marble portico of the Bethlehem Pedersen Hotel, Simon pointed across the artificial lake to another giant hotel. It was called Herod's Palace. Built similar to the archeologist's drawings of Herod's summer palace near Jericho, it was complete with hanging gardens, numerous spas and mineral baths, and featured a disco where Salome was already dancing nightly for enchanted customers.

The Bethlehem Pedersen, where they were standing, was far more traditional. It featured a kindly "innkeeper." Inside the lobby was a replica of the cave where Jesus was born. Tours would be available throughout the day for registered guests to go through the man-made grotto.

The three men boarded a moving sidewalk. A special guide appeared and narrated the *story* of Jesus' birth. She pointed out the angels hovering over a far-off field. Shepherds made their way toward the inn where robots Joseph, Mary, and baby Jesus moved in lifelike form in the stable. Rounding a turn, Panther almost bumped into three Eastern kings on mechanical camels. The kings asked the guide if she knew where the baby was born, for they had been following a star for a number of nights. Turning toward the grotto, the guide pointed to the star, shining its ultraviolet light down on the manger scene.

"We need both hotels," Jessup told Panther. "For those who want to dance the dance of the seven veils with Salome and for those who want to follow a star. Remember," he added, "many of the people coming to Jesus World will not be Christians. We want to provide them the entertainment they are used to so they will come back and bring their friends."

Joe Panther glanced quizzically at Pedersen. Jessup resumed his description as the men moved from the hotel toward the park entrance.

"Guests can go by several means into the park," he said "They can use the moving sidewalks, monorails, our underground subway which enters the city through Hezekiah's tunnel, or this new transportation system known as 'Electro- mover,' which allows people to ride these free-floating capsules on powerful tractor beams into the heart of Jesus World."

"Tickets will be sold at the front gate," Pedersen added "Besides the cover charge, which allows them to enter the gate, there will be additional tickets to allow the spectators to enter a number of side attractions. It will take a minimum of three days for a family to visit every attraction."

"The main attractions," Jessup pointed out, "are the reenactment of the Crucifixion and the Resurrection. These will be limited to Wednesday and Sunday, coming as a climax to those who have been in the park the three days preceding."

"You're going to crucify Jesus all over again?" Panther asked. It was more of a statement than a question, but Pedersen winced.

"Thousands of camping spaces are ready, in addition to Simon's two hotels," Jessup continued. Tickets are being sold through churches around the world and at special Jesus World ticket booths in major airline terminals and even on Times Square in New York City where opera tickets are sold."

The trio moved slowly into the park where workmen were busy with last minute details. "Here at the front gate the spectators will group into 'congregations' of 70 'members,'" Bert intoned.

"You'll appreciate that, Panther. We're thinking big but wanted you to know that we still hold to the principles of small groups."

Joe said nothing. Instead, he gave a slight Indian-sounding grunt, as Jessup resumed his narration.

The pilgrims, as the spectators were called, bunched in groups of 70, would be ushered by the robed "apostle" -- a real-life young man of sterling personality -- onto the waiting Electro-mover. As the next "congregation" formed behind them, the first group would be whisked quickly to the left before disembarking at the first attraction: The Garden of Eden.

"We can't activate all the attractions yet," Simon said. "But the people sitting in this giant theater will be surrounded by quadraphonic sound and sky projectors. The entire panorama of Creation will take place around them. There will be a dazzling spectacle with a light show highlighting the creation of heaven and earth. The mighty roar of waters will be heard as floodgates open and the seas flood the arena. Overhead, galaxies will burst into being, suns will explode, comets will roar past and suddenly dry land will emerge. The seas are controlled by these huge valves which drain them as the mountains rise from the midst of the waters. Then animals, all robots of course, will appear -- just as a rumbling voice speaks: "Let us make man after our image, in our likeness ....'

"A misty finger will stir the dust and a robot Adam will arise from the earth, standing fully erect. As he stretches, the fog encircles him, and emerging from the other side, her back to the spectators, is Eve. They'll embrace as the lights dim and the people are escorted from their seats to the next attraction."

"It's time," Jessup said, "to put an end to the teaching of evolution. But to convince people of the genuineness of the single Creation, we have to make it exciting."

Panther grunted again and dropped back behind Jessup as they continued the tour.

"From, the Garden of Eden, they stepped aboard the waiting computerized Electro-mover and were whisked to Noah's Ark. Entering the huge ark, they were surrounded by hundreds of Muppet-like animals. High above was the robot Noah, seated on the balcony at the top of the pitching and tossing zoo. Jessup threw a switch and the robot moved to open a window. A robot dove flew in with a green twig in its beak.

"We expect the crowd to cheer when that happens." Jessup said with a grin. "I only wish I could show you the rainbow, but it won't be ready until opening day."

They moved on to the Tower of Babel. Technicians were running a final check so Panther got to see it in action. He could hear the roaring voice of God as the majestic structure collapsed. Robot workers scattered -- babbling in different languages. Then another switch was thrown and the stones, drawn by magnetic waves, swiftly flew back to their original place in the tower, ready for the next group of pilgrims.

They moved then to the back side of the property, where bulldozers and earth movers had created Mt. Sinai with its triple peaks. "You need to go up there to really see what it's like," Jessup said to Panther.

"I'll take your word that it's unbelievable," Joe

said quietly.

Jessup continued. "Inside the mountain, viewers can board a rapid-speed elevator to the peak. Stepping out on a small platform, they will see a bearded robot, the exact image of Michelangelo's Moses. Artificial lightning flashes will shower the mountain with sparks and in the rumbling thunder the pilgrims can distinguish the voice of God. The robot Moses will pick up two stones and red laser beams will burn Hebrew letters into the tablets."

"Come with me," Simon said excitedly. "I want you to see this."

Following a robot Joshua, the three men marched up to the walls of the ancient city of Jericho. "When this happens next week, the Jordan River will open before them," Bert said. Surrounded by rugged Israeli troops -- all robots -- the three walked around the replica of the city. At one place on the city wall, Rahab, with her red ribbon, waved down at them. Joshua thundered his orders to spare her since she protected the Israeli spies. Suddenly giant cracks appeared in the walls. Stones tumbled and Styrofoam walls came crashing down under the direction of internal machinery. The troops of Joshua rushed into the city.

"What do you think?" Simon asked

"It's impressive," Panther admitted. Then he added, "I only wish all walls came down that easily."

"It's done through the miracles of science and technology," a strangely accented voice said from behind them.

The men turned around. The chief engineer, Yosef Ben-Korach, was leaning on the immobile Joshua robot.

"Old Joshua couldn't begin to bring down those

walls without the power of a computer -- and a lot of miracle-working engineering," the handsome Jew laughed.

Bert Jessup stepped forward and introduced Panther to his chief engineer.

"So you are the miracle worker," Joe Panther said, looking at the dark-skinned man with twinkling eyes and black, curly hair.

"The problem with miracles," Yosef said as he pushed back his construction worker's hard hat, "is they never can be predicted. I don't know much about God. But if I were God, I'd never let anyone know when I was going to do a miracle. If people knew when He was going to do it, they'd eventually figure out how He did it, and that would make them God. I'll leave that for the 'Reverend' here to figure out," he said, pointing at Jessup.

"But we need predictability here at Jesus World," Yosef continued. "Nothing's left to chance or happenstance. We're having enough trouble with the county building inspectors as it is. They're afraid one of our robots might get out of control. So we've programmed all our miracles to happen on cue."

"Yosef's the finest engineer in the world," Bert explained. "I predict that sooner or later he'll become a follower of the Messiah."

"We've got 48 Messiahs in the park," Ben-Korach laughed. "You just tell me which one to follow, and I'll do it -- as long as I get to push the buttons."

Jessup and Pedersen laughed. Panther's face was straight as he said, "You ought to feel right at home in most of today's churches."

When Yosef Ben-Korach pulled Jessup aside to check out a few last minute details, Panther quickly turned to Simon.

"Do you know what the Bible means when it says: 'Walk not in the counsel of the ungodly'?"

Simon shook off the question. "Yosef is the best design engineer in the world. You have to have a man with such gifts in a project like this."

"This son of Korah may be a genius, but he's also a cynic, a nonbeliever," Panther pursued. "He has no understanding of spiritual things."

"Joe, we're praying for him every day. It takes talent to build something like this. If the lord is in charge of it. He will overrule the unbelievers."

"But Simon, is the Lord really in charge here?"

"We're going ahead on the basis that He is," Pedersen said firmly.

The men resumed their tour, leaving Ben-Korach to finish his work on the walls of Jericho. There were more than 100 separate attractions, each true to the biblical story. For a few dollars, visitors could see Delilah cutting Samson's hair and watch as the Philistines blinded him and chained him to the giant pillars in the meeting hall. At the end of the show, Samson, crying out to God, pulled down the pillars on his enemies.

In another section the young shepherd boy David, who was so lifelike it was hard to believe he was a robot, guided the men around a huge rock and brought them face to face with a roaring Goliath. David threw a stone just in time and the huge giant collapsed at the feet of Bert Jessup.

They boarded the monorail over Prophet's Land. Below could be seen the roaming prophets. There was Amos tending his sycamore trees. Hosea was at the slave market, bidding to purchase his wife Gomer from the block. Disembarking, they stood over the Valley of Dry Bones and heard

Ezekiel prophesying to the wind. Jessup threw a switch and the bones came alive, flying through the air to join together. Through the marvels of holographic projections, flesh seemed to appear, and the bones formed into a mighty army, marching out of the valley as the prophet stood on the side of the mountain with his staff raised.

The men moved on to the right side of Jesus World where the New Testament attractions were located. Jessup was especially eager to show them the Garden of Gethsemane. It was located just below the Temple Mount. Plastic olive trees, so real looking even Ben-Korach's visiting friends from Israel had been fooled, gave a feeling of peace and tranquility. There was a robot Jesus kneeling beside a huge rock. Bert pointed where the ushers, dressed in biblical clothing, would ask the pilgrims to be seated and motion them to silence.

"Ever since I built my first Garden of Gethsemane," he said, "with those cheap wax figures, I've dreamed of something like this. Now it has come to pass."

His eyes were moist as he paused, looking around the beautiful garden. "Here people will be able to see Jesus in His agony, His suffering. They will enter and sit reverently around the garden. Over there are the apostles asleep. Behind the trees will be seen the torches and lanterns of the Roman soldiers coming to arrest the Master. As Jesus kneels at the rock, praying, drops of blood appear on His forehead and drop to the ground. No one will leave this garden dry-eyed."

Next came the Temple, overshadowing everything. The men entered on moving sidewalks and took escalators to the viewing level. Below, at the Gate Beautiful, they saw where Peter and John robots would heal the man lame from birth.

In the outer court, Bert explained how some of the pilgrims would be part of a frenzied and fearful mob of money-changers, fleeing in front of Jesus (played by an actor) with a whip in his hands. Mechanical pigeons and sheep would scatter in all directions.

On the far side of the city stood Pilate's Court, the place of the *ecce homo.* It was there the trial of Jesus was to be reenacted. Beyond that, just outside the city wall, was Golgotha with its skull-like surface overshadowing the city below.

"Twice a week," Jessup said solemnly, "on Wednesday and Sunday, Jesus World will reenact the Crucifixion and Resurrection. The ceremony will begin at noon and climax at sundown. It is all done by electronics. I'll not try to describe it. You must see it to believe it. Following the Resurrection, which takes place in an amphitheater that is an exact replica of Gordon's tomb in Jerusalem, the people will be ushered to those twelve auditoriums." He was pointing to 12 buildings in a circle around the base of the Mount of Olives.

"There, I suppose, you take up the offering," Panther said evenly.

Simon could tell by the sarcasm in Joe's voice that the Indian was at the outer limits of his short temper span. Nervously he started to speak, hoping to avoid what might become a nasty scene. But Jessup was too excited over his description to detect Panther's mood.

"No offerings," Jessup said innocently. "Of course, we will give out materials so the people can make pledges if they want. We already have a number of wealthy people who are naming us in their wills. The Apostles' Auditoriums, however, are for the preaching of the Gospel. We have invited world famous preachers to come for a week at a time -- as guests of Jesus World. Each one will have a separate auditorium and will preach following the reenactment of the Resurrection. Our teams will hand out decision cards and assign counselors. We have thousands of preachers who have said they would like to come. We will give out follow-up packets and recommend these people to local churches all over the world."

Panther pointed at the little shops on the cobblestone streets. "What are these?"

"Everything imaginable," Jessup laughed. "One is our first aid station. Another is our security headquarters, manned," he chuckled, "by the Praetorian Guard of Caesar's army. The rest are concession stands. We've already sold franchises to firms who will sell ancient coins, full length prophet's robes, even Elijah's mantle, singed around the edges from the fiery chariot. Pilgrims like to purchase souvenirs. These will be prayer reminders so they can pray daily for Jesus World."

"What kind of reminders?" Panther asked

"All kinds of things. There are items like Moses' staff, tiny jars of manna, Peter's sword with which he cut off the ear of the servant of the high priest, the dice the Roman soldiers threw at the base of the cross, even a Burning Bush Night Light for your bedroom."

"Shades of the Dark Ages," Joe Panther muttered.

Later that night Simon had a telephone call from Joe Panther.

"I had to call you, Simon, because my conscience has been troubling me ever since I left you and Bert this afternoon."

"What's troubling you, Joe?"

"Jealousy, I guess. I acted badly today and I'm sorry. Some of those cracks I made about Bert were inexcusable. He's done a fantastic job. I was impressed in spite of myself."

"That's great to hear, Joe. Then we can count on your support."

There was a pause at the other end. "Simon, I can tell you in all honesty that the creativity of Jesus World impresses me. I can offer my help and support to you as a friend, but the 'extravaganza for Jesus' approach will never be my way. Be careful, Simon. It can get out of hand."

"Thanks, Joe, for your call -- and advice. You mean a lot to me. I want to come back to the ranch soon and get my body in shape again."

"I hope you will, Simon." Joe's voice was wistful.

VIII

INSTEAD OF TWO YEARS, it took Jesus World exactly one year after it opened to break into the black, bringing the hope of a huge return for those who had invested money. Instead of declaring a profit, however, Jessup convinced his board they should invest the money in new projects such as the Ascension and Second Coming which were now possible through electronics.

The board was too overwhelmed at the success of the project to object. Religious leaders from across the world were giving their endorsement. Many of them received expense-paid invitations to come as Jessup's guests to the Bethlehem Pedersen and were given the red carpet treatment on a tour of Jesus World. All returned singing its praises.

Problems had arisen however with local church leaders. Jessup had assured them the multitudes of people who would flock to the area could mean only prosperity for the nearby churches. He had even hinted a tithe of the profits from Jesus World would go back to the churches in the vicinity. However, the profits were now being reinvested in expansion, and for some reason the people who came to Jesus World never seemed to get around to attending the local churches. Not only that, but Jessup had neglected to tell the pastors the climax of the week's activities would take place on Wednesday and Sunday -- the very days the churches had their own meetings.

Yet the local pastors could not object too strenuously as they heard and saw the results of the ministry. More than a quarter of a million people a week were streaming into Jesus World. Of these, thousands were reported to have made first-time decisions for Jesus Christ. The ministry in the Apostles' Auditoriums was constant revival. Countless numbers were returning to the world claiming to have seen the reality of Christ through Jesus World. Despite the fact there was no way to follow up on these people, or to see that they were established in churches, no one could deny Bert Jessup had become the best known religious figure in America.

One of his new projects was the Celestial City Restaurant with "heavenly food." The restaurant towered above the park on top of David's Citadel inside the old city wall. It rotated once an hour so diners could see the entire park. Huge "angel capsules" rose and descended on tractor beams called sky-vators, carrying excited diners to the top.

Reservations for the Celestial City during the Sunday and Wednesday hours of the Crucifixion and Resurrection were booked a year in advance -- at $150 a plate.

There were a number of smaller eating establishments around the grounds. Elijah's Widow served breakfast of pancakes and syrup. Pilgrims could also purchase a cruse of oil from her to take home and serve their own pancakes and syrup. Unfortunately, Jessup was unable to design a cruse -- like the original one -- which didn't run dry.

Andrew's served loaves and fishes (fish and chips) from 12 different restaurants, all designed like woven baskets (for the 12 basketfuls left over from the feeding of the five thousand).

There was Mary and Martha's, with Mary acting as the smiling hostess and Martha serving up delicious food from her kitchen.

Of course, there was the exclusive seafood restaurant called Simon Peter's. Here, surrounded by nets, oars, and old fishing equipment, expensive seafood could be eaten leisurely while robot apostles mended their nets and a smiling Matthew tended the cash register.

The favorite with the children was Jonah's, a fast food place inside a concrete and fiberglass whale. Jonah, with seaweed in his hair, fixed hamburgers and French fries, and when the children finished eating they could sit in a spring chair which would (accompanied by a giant burp) swish them out of the fish's mouth.

But it was the extravaganzas -- those incredible miracles of electronics which dramatized the spectacular events at the close of Jesus' life -- which promised to draw the largest crowds ever.

Yosef Ben-Korach had convinced Jessup he should sink everything into electronics. It started with having robots replace the actors, including those playing the role of Jesus. "These new humanoids are so real you can hardly tell them from people. And they'll never forget their lines, grow woozy, or go on strike," Ben-Korach said.

At a cost of $100 million, Jesus World had put up a satellite. Nicknamed DEOSAT or "God Star," it was put into geosynchronous orbit around the earth 22,300 miles over the equator. Jessup explained to Simon that he would be able to rent out space on DEOSAT to religious organizations, including the Christian television networks. But more important, Ben-Korach pointed out, it could be tied in with Pedersen's giant computer in Belgium and, through programs developed there, could actually become the "brain" for Jesus World, controlling the robots and opening the door, finally, for the incredible extravaganzas Jessup had suggested for the Ascension and the Second Coming.

It was these last two events, now made possible by the hovering satellite, which catapulted Jesus World past all other amusement parks into worldwide attention.

Exactly one hour before sunset on Wednesday and Sunday, the Praetorian Guard began moving through the park, making sure all spectators were cleared from the Mount of Olives area. Then thirty minutes before the spectacular event of the Ascension was to begin, a magnetic fence surrounding the Mount of Olives was automatically activated by a sun-pumped laser signal from DEOSAT. This prevented anyone from entering the exposed sector. At that time an automatic countdown sequence began, counting down to the time when Jesus would suddenly appear on the top of the mountain. Clothed in white, standing almost eight feet tall, the Jesus robot began preaching to the crowds the last words of Christ on earth.

"All power is given unto me in heaven and in earth. Go ye therefore, and teach all nations, baptizing them in the name of the Father, and of the Son, and of the Holy Ghost...."

An unearthly hush fell over all Jesus World as the words thundered from the Mount. As the sermon ended, Jesus turned, looking up into the almost darkened sky in expectation.

Precisely at the time the sun reached three

degrees from the earth's horizon, DEOSAT, in orbit 22,300 miles above the earth, finished its final digital countdown. Powerful microwaves collected from the sun in solar cells hurtled from the satellite to the exact spot on the artificial Mount of Olives where the Jesus robot stood. These microwaves focused on the robot, which contained a rectenna. The rectenna converted the microwaves to electric current, activating a magnetic field. In a split second the entire top of the mountain glowed in an eerie light described in the literature as The Shekinah -- "The glory of God." For a long moment the robot itself glowed, then slowly disappeared as the light grew so bright it almost blinded the human eye. (Actually, it snapped back into its underground silo to emerge again at the next Ascension.)

But the exact image of the robot, reproduced by photo-electronics in a process called "molecularizing" -- a derivation of the holographic projections used by Disney World in their Haunted House attraction -- appeared in a gaseous form out of the blinding light. Translucent, yet dearly visible in every detail in the twilight, the ghostly form, glowing brightly, began to ascend, pulled heavenward by the tractor beam from DEOSAT. The higher it rose, the bigger it became until at 20,000 feet it seemed to fill the entire sky. At 30,000 feet, six miles above the surface of the earth, it caught the final rays of the sun and exploded into a kaleidoscope of color, disappearing into a huge, artificially induced rainbow which filled the whole sky until the sun disappeared beyond the horizon.

Suddenly another holographic image, activated by the laser beams from DEOSAT, appeared, hovering over the entire park site. The angelic image, dressed in flowing white robes and seemingly suspended by feathery wings, spoke these words from Acts: "Ye men of Galilee, why stand ye gazing up into heaven...."

Then, slowly, the angel ascended the same tractor beam to DEOSAT. The next laser signal from the satellite deactivated the magnetic safety fence and the people were once more free to move about the park.

Jessup's only problems with the Ascension, interestingly enough, were not technical. Rather they came from the county building and safety inspectors. The local officials were already in a quandary over what to do with Jesus World. On one hand it *was* bringing in more money than the little county had ever imagined existed. At the same time, however, the accompanying problems were almost more than they could cope with. New roads, new schools, new utility plants, a new hospital -- and now, a safety hazard that they simply did not know how to handle. The building inspector, realizing the incredible dangers of microwave beams converging on a small area where tens of thousands of people were gathered, had no choice but to threaten to force Jessup to quit using the satellite. Jessup's own engineers had warned him of the danger of microwaves from a satellite -- especially those of the intensity necessary to create the electronic miracles. "Anyone who gets in their way will be fried like a piece of bacon in a microwave oven," he was told.

Jessup turned the matter over to his chief engineer, Yosef Ben-Korach, and told him to work it out with the county officials. "Do anything you have to do that's legal," he said. "If they don't let us use our satellite, we're in big trouble. I mean big trouble."

Yosef grinned "You need a miracle? Trust me, Bert. You'll get one. I'll show you where real miracles come from. They come from the brains of men."

That same afternoon, Yosef Ben-Korach met with the county officials. At his request, the county commissioners were present also. He wanted to make them an offer they couldn't refuse.

"Before we talk about the satellite," Ben-Korach began, "I understand you're facing some impossible problems caused by Jesus World."

The commissioners all nodded in agreement. Yosef continued. "As a gesture of our good will, we want to help. Bert Jessup has authorized me to take over all the expenses for the widening and paving of all major thoroughfares in the county. That includes building new roads, new bridges, and payment to relocate any families inconvenienced by the construction. We also want to build a new school, named after the chairman of the county commission."

Following that, there was very little talk about the safety regulations regarding the Ascension. The county commissioners agreed that Jesus World occupied a special place and was, indeed, almost a separate county. Yosef explained how the magnetic fence was fail-safe. If it did not go up, the satellite would not activate the microwaves at sundown. He also agreed that on days where there were exceptionally large crowds their own security force -- the Praetorian Guard -- would not only personally clear the area, but they would form a human fence, linked arm in arm, around the entire Mount of Olives until the magnetic field was activated. That satisfied the county commissioners, who did not even give the building inspector a chance to speak.

The meeting was dismissed and Ben-Korach had his secretary bring in the special gifts for each of the commissioners, which included not only a case of whiskey each, but special passes for the commissioners and their families to all Jesus World attractions.

"Stay close to me," Ben-Korach told Jessup when he reported the good news that evening, "and I'll show you how miracles are done."

By the end of the year other extravaganzas were in operation. In a called conference in Jessup's office with Simon Pedersen present, Ben-Korach outlined his proposal for the Second Coming.

"For this miracle," he laughed, looking at Simon with twinkling, jet-black eyes, "we have no predictability. I am taking a software program designed by your Belgian computer and programming it into the brain of DEOSAT. From then on everything becomes automatic."

"I thought you said all your 'miracles' had to be predicted?" Simon asked.

"All but this one, Simon," Jessup said seriously. "Yosef has agreed that for this one event we should take hands off."

"There will be no forewarning," the Jewish engineer said to Pedersen. "It will always come as an utter surprise."

"That coincides with the Bible," Jessup said. "'It is not for you to know the times or the seasons....'"

"The only thing we are sure of," Yosef said, lighting a cigarette and leaning back in his chair, "is the Second Coming will always come the last week of the month between the hours of 11 p.m. and midnight."

"That gives people time to finish with most of the attractions," Bert said. "We wouldn't want their money-spending to be interrupted by the Second Coming."

Yosef got up from his chair and went to a mounted drawing board which had been covered with a cloth. Removing the cloth, he revealed sketches of DEOSAT over Jesus World.

"Signals from DEOSAT will set off laser beams that will flash across the sky. This will activate numerous holographic projections giving the appearance of the clouds rolling back. As you know, we have recently purchased two homopolar electric generators, built in Australia especially for us. These machines use two rapidly spinning flywheels to build up and store electricity. In one second the Canberra homopolars can deliver 500 mega joules of direct current -- enough to light the City of Orlando. These brilliant flashes of light, activated by the lasers from DEOSAT, will go spitting and crackling through the heavens, creating not only artificial lightning storms that send daggers of light from east to west, but they will recreate something dear to you -- the shimmering optics of the *aurora borealis*."

"The northern lights," Pedersen smiled, remembering those magnificent displays along the Arctic Circle when he and his stepfather would stand on the deck of the rolling fishing boat and see all the colors of the spectrum flash across the sky.

Yosef grinned at Jessup and continued "In the midst of this spectacular light show of flashing lasers, there will be the sound of a thousand trumpets, including the blast of the *shofar*." He paused, looked at Simon and said, "That's the traditional Jewish ram's horn."

"You keep forgetting I was a Jew long before Israel was a nation," Simon said. "No need to explain the *shofar* to me."

"Of course," Yosef said. "Sometimes I overstep myself."

"But the best is yet to come, Simon," Jessup said, getting up and moving toward the drawing board. "In the middle of all this display of light and sound, the white-robed figure of Christ will appear in the eastern sky -- 60,000 feet in the air -- accompanied by angels and holographic projections of all the biblical figures the people have seen during the day at Jesus World. There will be Adam and Eve, Noah, Moses, the prophets, David, the apostles. It will happen 12 times a year, computed electronically by the brain in DEOSAT. That's symbolic, since only God knows the time. On a clear night you'll be able to see it all over the state of Florida, as far south as Cuba, even to the Bahama Islands -- Christ coming in the clouds."

"Think of it, Simon," Bert said, his hands opening and closing in excitement, "everyone within a 200-mile radius will know that Jesus is coming again. Joe Panther was right about one thing, Simon, Yosef Ben-Korach is indeed a miracle worker."

IX

THE LATE AFTERNOON SUN was a fireball, its rays filtered, however, by the overhanging branches of the giant oaks at Koinonia Ranch. The two men, Simon Pedersen and Joe Panther, sat on small concrete benches under the spreading branches. Gray Spanish moss hung from the trees, allowing only occasional shafts of the sun to enter, making little designs on the small patches of grass underneath. It was a quiet afternoon. The men in the ranch program were picking vegetables and the women were at work in the canning plant. A few honeybees from nearby hives buzzed through the oak and moss cathedral where the men sat talking. Joe got up from the bench and squatted, Indian style, resting his back against the rough bark of a water oak.

"The sights and sounds of Jesus World overwhelm us here," he said bluntly.

"Maybe we need to find you another place," Pedersen replied.

"It's not that," Joe said sadly. "Something just seems wrong at the heart of all this. How can we make Jesus personal, how can He heal the brokenhearted, give sight to the blind, open prison doors and raise the dead – when all this is going on?"

"Jesus World has become huge all right,"

Pedersen was saying. "But is that necessarily wrong? For once in my life, Joe, I have found something I can pour myself into. And there are times when I think God must be quite proud of what we are doing."

The two men were silent a moment pondering the situation. Jesus World was more than three years old, a success in every way. Joe had known for the past year that if he voiced any objection it would sound as if he were threatened by this success. But things were not going well at his ranch. That was the reason he had asked his old friend, the Silver Fisherman, to meet with him.

"Simon," he said softly, "we've known each other for a number of years. I've always tried to be honest with you. Love is synonymous with speaking the truth. I would be less than a friend, indeed I would be your worst enemy, if I did not ask you some honest questions."

"That's why I've come, Joe," Simon said seriously. "I know you have had serious objections, and I want to help you work them out."

Joe took an oak twig and traced circles around a little mound of dirt at his feet, as though to make a road for the doodlebug in the sand to climb to the peak and peer across the landscape.

"Do you think God has changed His method since the days of Jesus?" he asked.

"What do you mean?"

"Jesus seemed to feel the way to win the world was to take a few men and make disciples of them," Joe said, still doodling with his stick in the sand.

"I asked this question of Bert Jessup years ago, Joe. The answer that has come to me is that God wants us to use every method at our disposal to win people to Him. When Jesus was on earth He walked because He had no car. He never traveled abroad because there were no airplanes. He lived in a limited world and used limited methods. But we are unlimited. God has revealed to men countless ways to spread the Gospel. We're using many of them at Jesus World and producing a staggering number of decisions for Jesus."

A slight smile played over Panther's face. He reached up and pushed back his sweat-stained cowboy hat, rocked back in his squatting position, and dug the heels of his scuffed cowboy boots, crusted with cow manure, into the sand. His voice was now soft, like the whisper of an Indian canoe sliding through the silky water of the Everglades.

"When the Children of Israel were wandering in the wilderness *every* need was met. They had free food every morning that fell from heaven. Their shoes and clothing did not wear out. When they were without water, it came gushing from the rocks...."

"They were under God's blessing and provision," interjected Simon.

"Ah, but there is a difference between blessing and provision. Provision means you have your needs met. Blessing means you have ample to give to others. Those Children of Israel were totally out of the will of God. They were a doomed people, doomed to wander until *every* adult was dead."

"What are you saying?" Pedersen asked, his voice on edge.

"I'm saying," Panther said, standing to his feet, taking off his hat and running his hand through his long black hair, "That I think you are making a mistake to stay involved with this man -- Jessup -- and with his project. I'm convinced that neither are of God."

"But Joe," Simon asked intently, "didn't Jesus tell us to go and teach all nations? We're doing that at Jesus World. In fact, we're going one step beyond. We're bringing all nations to us. This last year we had representatives -- I mean official government representatives -- from 87 nations. They tell us that Jesus World is the biggest thing to happen to Christendom since Constantine declared the Roman Empire to be under the sign of the cross and marched his armies through the river to baptize them."

A slight smile played over Panther's olive-skinned face. His black eyes closed gently. "Much of our present trouble started with Constantine. He tried to Christianize a secular society by mass proclamation. He wound up commercializing the Kingdom of God. It was he who gave us the state church. The same mistake was repeated in the Crusades and attempted by some of our New England forefathers. You cannot mix the methods of this world's system with the concepts of the Kingdom."

He paused a moment, then took the plunge. "Simon, I believe you are being sucked into the whirlpool. You are a genius of an entrepreneur, but totally untrained in theology and naive about most spiritual matters. You are repeating the mistake so many energetic business men make of thinking you can transpose your worldly methods of making money into enterprises for the Lord. The Apostle Paul did that in his early ministry and had to be ushered out of Damascus and later Jerusalem until he could learn to follow the Holy Spirit, not his old traditions."

"Then you think Jessup is Satan's tool not God's." Pedersen's eyes were flinty, his voice clipped.

"I think that Bert deeply and sincerely believes God has anointed him and Jesus World. It is now his whole life, and he's convinced I'm jealous and resentful of his success."

"Are you?"

Joe sighed. "I know I sound that way. I prayed all last night about this get-together with you, Simon. I asked Jesus to remove the hostility in me toward Bert. It was there, I admit it. I thanked Him for all the people who have come to Christ there at Jesus World. Then I thanked him for Bert's creativity. Finally, I thanked God for Bert himself."

Simon's taut face relaxed. "If I believed that Jesus World was playing into Satan's hand, I'd pull out in a minute."

Joe Panther reached into the upper pocket of his cowboy shirt and took out a small worn Bible. "If you read this Greek New Testament, you will find that Jesus did not tell His followers to go and teach all nations. What He actually said was 'Go and make disciples of all nations.' There is a vast difference. That means more than *evangelizing*. It means *enlisting* men and women into the ways and means of the Kingdom. Use the word 'teaching' if you want, but remember, if you teach it means to make pupils. I do not see how you are doing that with Jesus World. You are not making disciples. I think you are only bringing in the sheep, shearing them of their protective wool, and then covering them with something much more synthetic."

Pedersen chuckled "Joe, you are always surprising me. For a man who grew up in a teepee, you are splashing about an awful lot of theology."

Joe's eyes suddenly flashed "I'm not trying to snow you with my Greek. I believe with all my heart that Bert and his circus will bring you misery and despair. And I...I get angry because you are my Christian brother and I deeply care what happens to you."

Both men were silent for a while, then Joe added softly, "Besides, I didn't grow up in a teepee -- it was a wickiup."

When Simon returned to his office, there was a message for him to call Bert Jessup. It was labeled urgent. His secretary soon had Jessup on the phone.

"What is it, Bert?"

There was a sigh at the other end of the line. "Bad news, I'm afraid The Internal Revenue Service has ruled against us. They say we're not a church, so we can't accept contributions.

"What will that cost us?"

"I don't know yet. Our lawyers say it could run a hundred million or more."

"Ouch! I assume we will appeal."

"They think it would be better if Jesus World actually became a church."

"A church! How is that possible?"

"By filing to become a tax-exempt 501(c)(3) corporation. After all, Jesus World really is a church. It is doing more for people than all the churches in Florida."

Simon was silent for a long moment "Bert, we need to give this a lot of thought."

X

ON MARCH 15 of its fourth year, Jesus World became a church. Officially. After considerable resistance at first, Simon capitulated when he saw the latest financial report. With so many new and costly projects undertaken, expenses had climbed above income. The IRS ruling had put them in a bad cash flow position. Something had to be done.

To meet the requirements of being a church, their organization needed a membership. Jessup used the occasion to announce his newest plan, "Jesus World Partners." All those who contributed $1,000 a year became partners, or members. They were allowed to wear the official Jesus World lapel pin, shaped like the satellite DEOSAT, which had become the official logo for the park. They were also allowed unlimited free entrance through the main gate of Jesus World and received a 50 percent discount off all attractions inside the park except the restaurants, hotels, and concessions.

In order to distinguish between members and non-members (there were tens of thousands from all over the world who wrote out their annual contribution check the first time they visited Jesus World), Jessup devised an idea where a small, painless, invisible tattoo was placed on the inside of the right thumb, opposite the thumbnail, of all who became partners. As Moses anointed the right thumb of the Levites before they were allowed to enter the sacrificial area of the Tabernacle, so members of Jesus World were sanctified by the invisible tattoo on the right thumb.

The tattoo could be read only by a robot which stood at the front gate. When a thumb was pressed against a glass plate held in the robot's hand, a scanner flashed a signal to an interior computer where all membership records were stored. In a fraction of a second the computer verified the information and determined if the partner was current in his contribution. If he qualified, the robot would then activate a special gate so the member could pass through without having to stand in line, and would issue him a card good for the 50 percent discount on that particular date.

Shortly after the partnership plan went into effect, Yosef Ben-Korach suggested they give a biblical name to the robot who sat at the entrance of the gate screening members from non-members. One of the technicians suggested he be named Gabriel, after the famous angel who made the announcement to Mary of the coming Messiah. Another suggested he should be called St. Peter, who, according to tradition, sits beside the pearly gates in heaven checking credentials.

In the end, Yosef decided to send a signal through the master computer in Belgium, which in turn would send signals to DEOSAT. It had become a standing joke among the technicians that DEOSAT had replaced God. Phrases like "only DEOSAT knows" and "for DEOSAT'S sake" were commonplace among the workers at Jesus World. Big decisions always had to be cleared with DEOSAT. He literally controlled all the robots in the park and of course was the only one who knew the time of the monthly Second Coming. So it was only natural to send a signal to DEOSAT and ask him what they should name the robot at the gate.

The answer transmitted was *Golem.* No one understood, for the name had no meaning to any of the technicians – not even to Yosef. But DEOSAT was not to be questioned, so the robot which stood at the front gate admitting or barring those who wished to enter was called Golem.

XI

SIMON PEDERSEN, his eyes red from sleeplessness, called Joe Panther moments after the Pedersen Enterprises jet landed at the private strip outside Jesus World.

"I'm in trouble, Joe. I need your help."

It was an hour before sunrise, but Pedersen knew the schedule at Koinonia Ranch. Panther would be up working with the men in the kitchen preparing breakfast.

"I've just flown in from Atlanta. Mark is with me. Three days ago he almost died from an overdose of something called angel dust."

"High-powered dope." Panther said solemnly. "Sprinkled on marijuana or parsley and smoked. Can be a killer."

"Can you meet me in Ft. Pierce? I'm going to spend the day with him on the *Marah*. I need you along."

"I'll be there in a couple of hours," Panther said.

It had been more than a year since Pedersen had been aboard his expensive yacht. The hired crew had been faithful to keep it in perfect running order, taking it out on occasion to cruise up and down the Indian River (part of the Intracoastal Waterway that hugs the Florida east coast). But Simon had been too busy with the affairs of Jesus World to take any more of his "fishers of men" trips to the Bahamas. Now his world had come to a screeching halt with the telephone call from his chief executive officer that Mark had been found alone in his hotel apartment, near death from drugs. Hospital technicians had been able to pull him through, but Simon realized that Mark needed help, a lot of help. One suicide was enough for the Pedersen family. Business, even the Lord's business, must never again come before his son.

In fact, Simon worried, was it already too late? Mark had done such an excellent job at the Atlanta Pedersen that he had been made manager. But the added responsibility had obviously been too much. Mark had slipped back into his previous lifestyle. Now Simon prayed desperately he was not too late. Perhaps, he thought, the exposure to Jesus World would be the answer.

Then Simon realized that Mark first needed to be exposed to Joe Panther. That was the way it had happened to him. Maybe God would do it all over with his son.

Mark was asleep in the aft cabin when Joe Panther arrived on the *Marah*. The crew of the yacht had remained on board. Moments after Joe stepped on deck, the big diesels rumbled to life and the sleek boat pulled away from its berth in the marina, heading north up the inland waterway known as the Indian River. Although seas were calm that morning, Pedersen didn't want to go through the inlet at Ft. Pierce out into the ocean. He instructed his pilot to follow the channel markers up the beautiful Intracoastal Waterway to Vero Beach. He needed time to be with Panther, time to think, time to pray. The possibility of losing his son as he had lost his wife was almost more than he could face.

The two sat alone on the aft deck, sipping coffee from steaming mugs brought up from the galley by the mate. The shrimp boats were returning home from their night at sea, sloshing awkwardly through the rolling waters of the inlet, each one followed by a cloud of screaming gulls picking up bits of fish from the water as the sailors sorted through their night's catch. It was an overcast day, and both men were dressed in windbreakers. Panther, as always, was wearing his straw cowboy hat. Pedersen was bareheaded, his silver hair tousled by the breeze which played over the water, forming little cats' paws of ripples. Within an hour the sun would be high in the sky and the men would doff their windbreakers and move under the canvas canopy in the shade. But now, in the early morning hour, they sat close together, drinking their coffee, talking quietly as the yacht plowed steadily through the gray water, past the landfill islands with their stately Australian pines, toward the more sparsely inhabited places of the river.

"What's gone wrong?" Pedersen asked, his red-lined eyes moist with gathering tears. "Last night, I found time to read my Bible for the first time in months. It opened to the Song of Solomon: 'They made me a keeper of vineyards, but mine own vineyard have I not kept.'"

Joe Panther leaned back in the deck chair, cupping his coffee mug in both hands. His eyes closed. Listening.

"I know," Pedersen continued, staring at the white wake behind the big yacht, "that the problem is not Mark. All he needs is direction. The problem is me. Someplace in me something has gone wrong."

His voice was choking as he continued. "I thought I had clear direction for my life when I left Koinonia. But it's been years since I've personally led anyone to Jesus Christ. I'm so involved in the business affairs of Jesus World there just hasn't been time. This boat..." and he had to pause to get control of his voice. "...the name comes from the springs of Marah in the Sinai that were bitter until touched by God...then...became sweet water. But now the water has become bitter again. Somehow I've departed from my first love. I want to find my way back. I want to find the right kind of branches to throw into the spring of my life to make it sweet again."

Panther began speaking, softly, deliberately. "For two years after I left the seminary I was the darling of the after-dinner circuit in Christian circles. I traveled the nation, speaking at every Jesus Rally, every convention, all the biggest churches. I was something of an oddity, a cowboy and an Indian all wrapped up in a Greek scholar who knew how to sway crowds through exceptional speaking ability. I was a constant guest on every Christian TV show in America. The first year I was a regular guest host on JCTV -- The Jesus Network show. I wore the powder blue suits. I had makeup applied *every* day for the noontime national show. I signed autographs. I had a ghost writer assigned to do my books. I even believed all those things people said about me, that I was a *very* important man in the Kingdom.

"But something diabolical was happening to me," Panther continued. "It was slow. Subtle. I relished the power and the respect. I enjoyed the huge paychecks. It was heady, to walk into some fancy clothing store and have the clerk know my name, or to catch a cab from the airport and have the cabbie tell me he saw my show the day before.

"But I was losing my worth as a human being. I was nothing more than a talking monkey before the camera or on the platform. I was invited to preach at the big rallies not because I had something to say, but because I was famous. When the lights were turned off, however, and the last amen was said, I went home and wept.

"It was during that time my wife left me. I began drinking. I was a fake, just like those robots at Jesus World. My life was controlled by things outside me: the program director, the platform committee, my booking agent. I was a fraud. A Christian fraud."

Simon Pedersen got up from his chair and walked to the edge of the deck, letting his fingers touch the plastic-covered nylon safety line which hooked to the gunwales. He stood for a long time, staring vacantly at the shore as it slipped by to the east. Just beyond the narrow spit of land lay the broad expanse of the Atlantic Ocean, hidden by the scrub palmettos and towering Australian pines. He turned back to the deck table and picked up his coffee mug, now empty, and ran his finger absently around the rim of the cup.

"What caused you to change, Joe? Why did you give it all up and return to reality? I've got to know, for deep inside I think I've made a mistake with my life."

"I was like a fish falling in love with the sun," Panther said, gesturing at the flopping mullet which broke the surface of the water in huge schools alongside the boat. "The air looks good from below. It's enticing. But if you linger in it, you die. I had to return to my habitat, or perish.

"I was captured by a simple statement in the Book of Mark," he continued, reaching into his shirt pocket for the ever-present Greek New Testament. "In the first chapter, Mark writes that Jesus called a small group of men to be *with* Him. That word 'with' is one of the biggest words in the Bible. Implicit in it is koinonia -- community. That word convinced me that to have a valid ministry, I had to be *with* people. It was not enough to preach at them. Everyone was doing that. I had to be with them. I didn't need an agenda or an order of service. All I needed was *koinonia*. Fellowship.

"Jesus began a movement that would be universal and last forever, yet He spent most of His time *with* a few men. So I determined I would spend the rest of my life with men. Working with them. Playing with them. Imparting to them all I know -- and am learning -- about God. That's the reason I am here today. I am directed daily as the Holy Spirit leads. He directed me, five years ago, to unsaddle my horse, drive my pickup to Orlando and take the bus to Chicago to tell you about Jesus. This morning He directed me to be with you on this beautiful yacht. All my life is spent being with people -- just as Jesus did."

"I believe in what you're doing, Joe. I also believe in Jesus World. If I'm wrong about this place -- and you seem to think I'm wrong for being involved -- then I've got to see it clearly. I feel somehow that my life -- and the life of my son -- is hanging in the balance."

The mate appeared with a fresh pitcher of coffee. Panther thanked him, took it from him, and refilled both mugs. Adding a tiny bit of sweetener, he stirred his cup and leaned forward in his deck chair, facing Simon.

"It's awfully easy for me to defend my ministry at Koinonia Ranch and make it sound like no one else is hearing from God. I've tried to be fair about Bert and not talk behind his back -- haven't always succeeded. But you and I are old friends, Simon, and I want you to know that what I say to you I will also repeat to Bert Jessup.

"I try to measure the success of groups not by their size, but by the spiritual climate." Joe continued. "Are they studying the Bible? Is there an awesome sense of worship? Is there a freedom for the Holy Spirit to take control? To manifest His gifts? Is there a desire to reach out to others? Is there a lack of self-righteousness -- and self-recognition? Is there a willingness for that entire ministry to die, that the Kingdom of God might flourish? These are some of the criteria for a successful ministry."

"I don't understand," Simon Pedersen said "If a ministry dies after it is born, how can that be successful?"

"Was Jesus a success?" Panther asked quietly, leaning back in his deck chair.

"Of course!"

"What was the greatest moment of His success?"

"The Resurrection!"

"I don't agree," Panther said, smiling. "That was the moment of greatest success for the Holy Spirit. For it was the Holy Spirit who raised Christ from the dead. The greatest moment of Jesus' success was when He submitted His body to be crucified. That was what He meant when He said to

Andrew and Philip just before His crucifixion: 'Except a grain of wheat falls into the ground and dies, it abides alone: but if it dies, it brings forth much fruit.'

"In the Kingdom, Simon, life always comes through death. It is an unalterable principle. If you want to find out if there is life in the seed, bury it. If it is a dead seed, it will simply rot in the ground. If it contains the life of the Spirit, it will sprout and produce many more seeds."

"Are you telling me I must die in order to live?" Simon asked solemnly.

"I can't tell you, for you must find your own way. I am saying the time is coming shortly when I shall die. Only then will we know if my seed has life and will sprout."

"But what about me?" Pedersen asked intently. "What is the right way for me?"

"Simon," Panther said looking straight into his eyes, "I have real problems with the humanistic assumption that we can find the 'right way' or the 'best way' to do everything. We Americans are constantly looking for a formula, believing if we follow it to the letter we'll get the desired results. It's the dynamics that are important, not the mechanics. Learn to listen to the Spirit and He will show you exactly what to do. My role in developing disciples is limited to imparting the Holy Spirit to those with me. I am not qualified to give directions for another man's life."

Behind the two men a hatch banged open. Both turned and looked. Mark Pedersen, his eyes blinking in the glare of the sun reflecting off the water, was standing in the hatchway. His black hair was tousled from sleep, his gaunt, hollow cheeks covered with a night's growth of dark whiskers. He paused in the passageway, then came out on deck.

"What century is this?" he said with a thick tongue. "I feel like I've just returned from a trip to outer space."

Joe was surprised how tall Mark was. His gangly body seemed to lumber rather than walk, his arms and legs stiff as though his joints were reluctant to bend. He wore thick, black-framed glasses. His hands were huge, like grappling hooks, yet his body was essentially thin, with narrow shoulders and narrow chest cavity. For some reason, he reminded Joe of a praying mantis -- slender but powerful. He was dressed in an expensive, but *very* rumpled, light tan business suit. His tie was pulled loose at the collar. He had left his shoes below and was standing in his stocking feet, blinking out over the calm water of the Indian River.

"Sit down, Mark," his father said with warmth -- yet with authority. "I want you to meet my executioner, Joe Panther."

XII

IT WAS PALM SUNDAY at Jesus World. The Crucifixion sequence beginning at 11 a.m. Sunday, had become the busiest day of the week with an average of 60,000 people in attendance. One Sunday in November it had outdrawn both the Tampa Bay Bucs and the Miami Dolphins, professional football teams. But it was the Easter period beginning the week before on Palm Sunday that the biggest crowds arrived. By ten o'clock already there were 65,000 people in the park. It was a record-breaking day.

There had been growing complaints from the churches in Central Florida, however, especially since Jesus World had become a legal church. Jessup had promised the pastors, who enthusiastically supported him in the beginning, that Jesus World would "draw people like flies" to the local churches. Many churches had built larger buildings to accommodate the anticipated crowds. The people had come, all right, but not to the churches. Instead they came by the millions to Jesus World. They came, and they brought their money. Again, not to the churches, but to Jesus World. The average family, reported *U.S. News and World Report,* spent almost $3,000 for the three-day visit to Jesus World. And that did not include the hotel fees, nor contributions which were now received on a daily schedule in the Apostles'

Auditoriums. Nor did it include the annual membership fee ("contribution" was the legal term, used to satisfy the IRS) which only recently had been increased to $1,500 a year -- with no complaints from the partners.

Earlier that Sunday morning, Joe Panther had made a special visit to see Bert Jessup in his office on the 8th floor of Herod's Palace. Jessup was eating breakfast at his desk. Alone. He knew he would be needed in the park, so he was getting an early start. Panther's visit was a surprise.

Joe was angry. Four of his men had been hired away from him by Jesus World. All were ranch hands -- rodeo riders. Over the last year Jessup had expanded his concept, which originally limited the attractions at Jesus World to biblical events. There was a hot air balloon attraction now, so pilgrims could float over Jesus World and see it from a vantage point in the sky. There was a steel drum orchestra from the Bahamas, "Ju-Jitsu for Jesus" entertainers from Asia, and the world famous "Flying Waldos" trapeze act -- "death-defying faith in action." Now from the heart of Florida's ranch land, a Jesus World Rodeo every Saturday night -- complete with the biggest names in country music from Nashville. It was this event that had lured the men from Koinonia Ranch.

"How can you say you are a church?" Panther demanded, struggling to control his temper. "The word 'church' in the Greek is *ekklesia* -- the 'called out ones.' It signifies a community, a fellowship, a family of people who do things together."

"We are a family, Panther," Jessup said calmly. "We have members all over the world."

"That's not a church," Panther grunted. "There

is a place for the legitimate ministries which support, supplement, and assist the local church. There are Christian universities, evangelistic organizations, even TV ministries. But you are different. You are sucking the life from churches by taking people, and their money, and using them as the Egyptians used the Jews as their slaves. You're not a parachurch, you're a surrogate church -- taking that which belongs to the Body of Christ and using it for your own ends."

"What do you want me to do, Panther?" Jessup asked. "Refuse to take the money when people actually thrust it at us?"

"Should a man refuse favors from another man's wife, even if she thrusts herself upon him?"

"Are you saying I am a spiritual adulterer?" Jessup snapped, pushing back his breakfast tray and wiping his mouth with an Irish linen napkin.

"That's your terminology, not mine," Panther said, his black eyes smoldering.

"Listen, Panther, people go where they are fed. They give their money where they are fed. The churches aren't feeding the people, we are. It's as simple as that."

"Not so," Joe said, his voice rising. "Offer a child cotton candy or a bowl of health food and he'll choose the candy every time. That's all you are giving these people -- cotton candy. It looks real, it tastes sweet, but it melts to nothing. There is nothing substantial about this entire program. And in the end it will rot their teeth, give them diabetes, and prevent them from wanting real nourishment."

"You always play the intellectual role and it makes me weary," Jessup said, leaning forward. "Know what you are Panther? You're a horse and buggy man -- or should I say pony and blanket man

-- in a jet age. If you were in charge of the Lord's work on this earth, you'd set it back 200 years."

"Wrong," Joe said. "I'd set it back 2,000 years."

Panther fought to stay in control. He was aware of how out of place his scuffed cowboy boots looked against the deep red pile of the carpet. He really didn't want to fight Jessup. He wanted to believe Jessup was not an evil man, just a misguided one. But how can you convince a man against his will? The night before, he had spent an entire hour on his knees in his little office at the ranch, praying the Lord would give him wisdom when he confronted Jessup. Yet all he had done was accuse him.

"I'm not here pleading the cause of the local churches," Joe said finally. "Most of them are as suspicious of me as they are of you. I'm simply saying God has not given up on the church, even though most of them have become social clubs rather than places of true relationship. Granted, the church may seem dead, but the Holy Spirit is still in the business of resurrecting the Body of Christ. Nor am I opposed to electronics, to TV, to satellites, the media, even a Jesus circus such as you have -- but for Christ's sake, do not make it into a god. Do not allow this modem Baal to rise above the people, enticing them to bow before it, to bring it tithes, for eventually it will do as Baal always does -- demand human sacrifice."

"Are you afraid the first blood might be yours?" Jessup asked, smiling slightly.

"You drew blood from me when you stole my men," Panther said, feeling the anger returning. "Did you know that last week an anguished father, carrying his eight-month-old

son with a waterhead and a horrible deformed
body, broke weeping past the security guards in
the 'Upper Room' and laid his baby on the Last
Supper table before your robot Jesus, crying,
'Master, heal my child!'?"

Jessup leaned back, propping his expensive
shoes on the top of his mahogany desk. "You
don't know the half of it. For weeks people have
actually been healed by reaching over
the ropes and touching my robots, Peter and John,
at the Gate Beautiful where they reenact the
healing of the man crippled from birth. And
yesterday an Arab princess, blind in one eye, said
she could see light after being at the Pool of
Bethesda. You can't argue with those results,
Panther. Especially when the princess got her father
to give Jesus World two million dollars."

"I do not deny miracles," Panther said his voice
now quivering. "God blesses faith wherever He
finds it. At Lourdes. At a tent meeting. In a home
group. Even in Jesus World. But you are
perpetrating a false gospel. You are the re-
emergence of Baal. You are Nimrod, raising a
Tower of Babel that is bringing great confusion to
the Kingdom. God will continue to bless His
people. But woe to the false shepherd who feeds
plastic to hungry sheep."

"I'm fed up with your accusations, Panther."
Jessup swung his feet off his desk and stood up, his
neck veins pulsating. "You tell me I am Baal, you
call me Nimrod, you criticize me for putting on a
rodeo that draws more on one Saturday night than
all your rodeos have drawn in 20 years put together.
Get lost, Panther. Go back to your cows and
cowboys."

As Panther stamped out of his office, Bert
Jessup stared after him morosely. The cowboy was
a constant burr in his side. An Indian intellectual --
what a combination! He knew that Panther would
be back, madder than ever. During the night Jessup
had ordered the lake, where Koinonia Ranch raised
their catfish, drained. He had discovered it was
partially on Jesus World property. All he had done
was drain his half, intending to fill it in for
additional parking. But when Panther discovered it,
there would be another storm. So let it blow. He had
much more important things to deal with.

Bert arose and paced the room. The financial
problems were serious. Much worse than Pedersen
knew. There was something almost diabolical
working against him. The trouble seemed to center
on Golem, the robot who checked the identification
of the partners. It had on regular occasions refused
entrance to some of their largest supporters. It was
as if the robot was deliberately trying to sabotage
contributions -- trying to make it harder for Jesus
World to receive money. This was the last thing he
needed -- a mechanical despot angering his most
faithful contributors.

There was a large delegation coming that
morning from Rhode Island, including five men
who were giving a million dollars each -- on an
annual basis. It would be just like Golem to refuse
them entrance.

Then there was the early morning call from
Simon requesting a meeting with him that very
morning. Simon had seemed upset. Though
beautiful outside, the weather inside Jesus World
was stormy.

The delegation from Rhode Island had entered
the park. As Jessup suspected, the only five people

Golem rejected were their large contributors.
Fortunately, Bert arrive in time to open the gate
manually, despite Golem's protest.

The idea of a robot being a deliberate
troublemaker angered Jessup. He wondered if the
signal was coming from DEOSAT, or if Golem
actually had some kind of malicious sense which
enabled him to interfere in the affairs of Jesus
World. It frightened him that he was even thinking
this way, for Bert Jessup had never questioned
God's power in his preaching and healing ministry.
Yet recently he had been listening more and more to
his close confidant, Yosef Ben-Korach. Yosef was
convinced that all miracles, even those in the Bible,
had some kind of logical, scientific explanation. He
had never tried to convince Jessup there was no
God, he simply explained with persuasive logic that
God did not interject Himself in the affairs of men.
His God had simply set the universe in motion and
put various laws in order. If man was smart enough
to figure out these laws, then he, too, could work
what seemed to be miracles. His prime examples
were the talking robots, the Ascension, and of
course the Second Coming -- all produced through
electronics.

It made some sense to Jessup. If Yosef could
produce these miracles now, who was to say that
some smart magician had not produced some of the
miracles of the Bible?

While Jessup could accept this rational
philosophy up to a point, he was at a loss to
explain what seemed to be supernatural powers --
evil powers -- now at work in his robot, Golem.
He decided he would reject that kind of thinking.
It was negative. It went against his whole
approach to life.

Jessup suspected why Simon sounded so upset when he called requesting the meeting. He had no doubt heard that new figures had been added to the holograms appearing in the Second Coming. Jessup had discovered there were people willing to pay huge sums of money if they could have a facsimile of their loved ones among those in the crowd of saints and angels accompanying Christ when He returned. Somehow this gave the remaining family a sense that all was right. It was a simple matter to build robots from pictures of those who had died, since all they had to do was shape the face and fit it to a robe. These did not even have to molecularize but could be projected through the sky projectors to the satellite where their images would be relayed to earth during the monthly Second Coming.

A few of the original angels had to be moved aside, of course, but Jessup felt it provided a genuine ministry to the families. There were various prices available, starting with a three-time appearance. For increased prices, the loved ones could be projected to appear twelve times. For those who paid the highest fee, they could be molecularized and permanently fixed in the crowd of returning saints.

The front line of those accompanying Christ, of course, belonged to the angels, the patriarchs, and the apostles. But Jessup quickly discovered people vying for positions in the second line of returning saints. Eighteen new faces had been added, including a Mafia figure and, while there was some criticism, the extra income seemed to justify everything. Jessup was certain he could explain it to Pedersen.

The two men met in the small office next to the computer room near the front gate. Simon Pedersen handed Jessup a document and then stepped over to a large plate glass window through which could be seen a score of tense technicians sitting before banks of black and white TV screens. Increasingly, things had been going awry in the park. A couple of robots had gone out of control. More and more, it seemed, the people in the park had been doing strange things. One man, for no accountable reason, had gone wild in the Temple and joined the robot Jesus in chasing the moneychangers from the outer court. On another occasion a young couple had tried to climb up on the cross with Jesus during the Crucifixion. As a result, Jessup had ordered a complete TV monitoring system installed so, from the moment you walked into Jesus World until you left, you were under surveillance by TV monitors who were in constant contact with the Praetorian Guard by walkie-talkie radio.

"Are you sure this is what you want?" Jessup asked, incredulous, after reading the legal document, properly notarized, handed him by Pedersen.

"I'm certain," Simon said. "I'm resigning from the board of Jesus World."

"But why, Simon? If I ever needed you, it is now."

"It's not just the tampering you're doing with sacred things," Pedersen said. "I do not want to make the same mistake with Mark I made with Cynthia. Had I resigned from Pedersen Enterprises earlier, she might yet be alive. Now I have let Jesus World become as much a god to me as my business was. If I'm to save my son, I must resign."

Jessup's face was pallid, his eyes sunken. Simon looked at him. He had changed markedly from the happy, excited, robust man of several years ago. It had been a long time since he'd heard Bert Jessup laugh -- although he used to laugh all the time. Simon felt sad. He didn't want to dessert his friend. At the same time, he knew the time had come to pull out.

"Simon, I can't let you do this." Bert's voice was desperate. "There are some things happening here -- financial things -- which you don't know about. We're in big trouble. I need you. Jesus World needs you."

Simon Pedersen shook his head. Once having made up his mind, he seldom changed it.

"This situation with Mark has convinced me I've let my values run amuck," Simon said. "Only this time I've become over-involved with religious activity. I want to support you, Bert, but I can no longer be involved."

He didn't mention it to Jessup, but a lot had happened in the week since Simon and Mark had talked with Joe Panther aboard the *Marah*. Before that first day on the yacht was over, Mark Pedersen had responded to Joe Panther's simple explanation of the Kingdom of God. He found it easy -- as his head began to clear from the near brush with death -- to realize he had no choice but to commit his life to Jesus Christ. The days following had been days of restoration between Simon and his son. They all had agreed that Mark should take a six-month leave of absence from his job and spend the time at Koinonia Ranch under Joe Panther, following the footsteps of his father.

At the same time, Simon Pedersen also made some decisions. He was going to let his vision for Jesus World die. To accomplish this he needed to get out. Much earlier, of course, he had deeded the property over to the new corporation. At that time, even though he remained in control of the property as chairman of the board, he had told the Lord the land belonged to Him. Now it was as if God was saying, "Since the land is mine, I want you to release it to me."

Simon concluded he had no choice, if he was going to be obedient to God, but to make a clean break. He had to resign from his position as chairman, resign from the board itself. He looked forward to returning to the *Marah* and taking up the simple ministry he had put aside to enter the exciting world of commercial religion.

"I've been doing a lot of looking around," Simon told Jessup as they worked their way through the masses of people pouring into the park, all wanting to get prime positions to view the Crucifixion. The two men were heading for the executive tunnel which would take them underground back to the corporate offices in Herod's Palace. "I see so many, like myself, caught up in religious works, moving too fast and crashing into the rocks. I want to spend the rest of my life, not skipping across the ocean going nowhere, but ministering as Jesus did -- to a few."

"I need you, Simon," Jessup said, the hint of panic returning to his voice. "I know we've not agreed on everything, but without you none of this would have been possible. I haven't told you, but we're faced with some big decisions. You know the IRS made us refund all those donations from the first three years before we became a church. Now, because of a crazy arrangement Ben-Korach made with the county commissioners, we're having to shell out millions of dollars to build all kinds of roads -- even a hospital. If we don't they'll shut us down because we're violating their stupid building codes. The Arabs have offered to put up the cash -- enough to pay all our debts. But only if I add Mohammed's figure on the front line of those returning with Christ during the Second Coming. We desperately need the money. If we don't get the Arab millions, we might have to close down. But if I compromise...."

"You've already compromised, Bert."

"Listen, Simon, I don't want to stand between you and Mark. But can't you put off this decision for another few months at least? The ministry of Jesus World is bigger than any family crisis. Mark is just one young man. What about these millions who need Jesus also? What happens to them if Jesus World closes down?"

The two men had disembarked from the private Electromover under Herod's Palace and were boarding the elevator to the 8th floor. Jessup took hold of Pederson's elbow. "People are coming from all over the world," he continued. "Last week more than 50,000 people accepted Christ. We received a phone call yesterday from the President of the United States *asking* if he could address the crowd on Easter Sunday about the moral values in America. I tell you, we have finally arrived. Don't let Satan blind your eyes, Simon. The Kingdom of God needs Jesus World. And Jesus World needs you."

"If Jesus World is to continue, Bert, my leaving will not make it fall. On the other hand, you need to determine just who has sent this financial crisis upon you. I don't want to find myself in a position of putting my finger in a hole that God dug in your dike."

"Stay, Simon," Jessup pleaded, his eyes frantic. "Just three months."

"I can't wait three months, Bert. My boy almost died last week. He needs me now."

"My God, Simon, that *boy* of yours is 31 years old!"

"But he's still my son. I was not the father I should have been when he was small because I was too busy with my business. Now I'm not a father because I'm too busy with the Lord's business. Both are sins. In fact, the latter may be worse than the former because I know better. Right now he's meeting me for lunch in my apartment. Then I'm going to escort him through the park. I'm eager for him to see the Crucifixion, the Resurrection, and the glory of the Ascension. He's never been here before, and now that he's a Christian this should have special meaning for him. The business is all yours, Bert. I only hope it won't possess you, as it almost did me."

Simon stepped back in the elevator. The door started to slide shut, but he pushed the "door open" button for a moment, checking its movement. "One last request, Bert. Remember our agreement concerning Koinonia Ranch. Even though that property belongs to the corporation, we agreed to let the ranch remain with Panther. I'm trusting you to honor that."

Simon released the hold button and pressed the button for the penthouse. Odd, he thought as the elevator slowed at the top floor, how things seem different once you've stepped aside. Just moments before he had been afraid of Jesus World. It seemed imperative that he get out -- or be crushed. But now he was free, he couldn't understand why Joe Panther seemed to think that the entire project was evil. Jesus World had been built for the glory of God. Untold numbers of people had been saved through the ministry.

Once inside his office he took off his silver and black jacket. He had played the role of the egomaniac long enough. No more black and silver clothes. No more "Silver Fisherman" image. By late afternoon he would be dressed casually. Next week he would be back on the *Marah,* with the sea splashing over the bow and the taste of salt on his lips, dressed in T-shirt, slacks, and tennis shoes. It was time to start living.

Meanwhile he was looking forward to the afternoon, escorting Mark through Jesus World. He realized his son had a long way to go. There had been two minor flashbacks from the drugs. The last occasion had been the worst, as Mark wandered around the penthouse apartment weeping and shaking. But it had passed, and with his dad to walk him through these next few days -- and with the promise from Joe Panther to work with him at Koinonia Ranch -- well, how could things go wrong?

XIII

JOE PANTHER JOINED SIMON and Mark for lunch in Pedersen's penthouse apartment. He was still angered over his confrontation with Jessup that morning and instead of returning to the ranch had been wandering around Jesus World feeling more and more oppressed. As they finished lunch, which had been catered by hotel room service, Simon, feeling free for the first time in years, began joking about Jessup's problems with the robot on the front gate.

"It's no joke," Panther said seriously. "Do you know who 'Golem' was in history?"

Simon put down his coffee cup. "Now, Joe, don't try to turn this into something evil. It's simply a short-circuit in the machine that's causing these problems -- not something supernatural."

Panther ignored Pedersen's attempt to placate. "Robots are basically demonic. The early Swiss alchemist, Paracelsus, who considered himself demonic, gave lectures on the creation of a homunculus and even offered a recipe of ingredients which would transform his creatures from machine to human. The recipe included human blood and putrefied semen."

"Come on, Joe," Simon said, a trace of agitation in his voice. "You're too hyped up about this. They're just machines."

"Hey, let him talk, Dad," Mark said, laying one

126

of his giant hands on his father's arm. "I think he's making sense. Anyone who has taken drugs knows there are demons. I want to know where these creatures come from. I've had them attack me too many times to deny the truth."

"Yes, but not in the form of robots," Simon argued.

Panther continued: "In the 16th century, a devout Jewish rabbi in Prague, Judah Loew, created a mechanical robot. It was supposed to protect the Jews from persecution. Legend has it that the creature came to life when a tablet with the divine name, *Shem,* was placed in its mouth. Later, when its masters tried to use it for unworthy purposes, it turned on its creators and destroyed them. The robot's name was *Golem.*"

"You mean Golem, like the robot who stands at the front gate?" Simon asked. "What a unique coincidence."

"It's no coincidence, Simon," Joe Panther said seriously. "The name came straight from that hovering satellite, a satellite which even the technicians in Jesus World admit has a mind of its own -- a super mind."

"Joe, you're talking about things I don't understand. I don't have any problem believing in a devil, but all this talk about machines taking on demonic characteristics turns me off."

"If Satan can possess a human being who has a will, why can't he possess a machine which has no will? Didn't his demons once possess an entire herd of swine in the cemetery at Gadara, causing them to run over a cliff into the sea?"

"It makes sense to me, Dad," Mark Pedersen said.

"What does the name Shem mean?" Simon

asked "You said the robot came to life when a tablet inscribed with that name was inserted in its mouth."

"Shem was one of the sons of Noah. Legend, again, links him with the world of the occult even in those early days. Even more interesting, however, is the fact Shem was the great-uncle of a man named Nimrod, who built the Tower of Babel. Babel, of course, was cursed and destroyed by God, but the spirit of Babel lived on -- the spirit of attempting to mold spiritual truths into political and economic form. Commercial religion, if you will. It took spiritual apostasy to design such a program, a program which later evolved into one of the most evil cities in history, a city which was a direct descendant of Babel – Babylon. This gave rise, by the way, to the worship of the god which combined the spiritual and the commercial, the most evil of all false gods, Baal.

"In the Book of Revelation, the Apostle John says he saw a whore sitting upon many waters, representing the nations of the world. There was a beast with seven heads and ten horns, and sitting on the beast was a woman with a name written on her forehead. That name was 'MYSTERY, BABYLON THE GREAT, THE MOTHER OF HARLOTS AND ABOMINATIONS OF THE EARTH.'"

"I don't understand," Simon said, his eyes fixed intently on Joe Panther's face.

"Mystery Babylon is that name equated in the World of God with spiritual apostasy, the refusal to believe the truth. I believe Bert Jessup is a modern day Nimrod. I believe Jesus World is a modern day Tower of Babel. It is the forerunner of another Babylon. Those who come are, unknowingly, worshiping Baal. I don't know how I can make it any clearer."

"I'm sorry, Joe," Simon said sincerely, "I just cannot accept that. Bert Jessup is a man of God. He loves Jesus Christ. He has been a great evangelist, used by God to heal and save untold millions. How can you call him Nimrod? He isn't building a tower to reach heaven."

"To create a living being is God's role," Panther said, standing and walking to the window overlooking the park "To assume God's role is blasphemous -- even diabolic -- and thus doomed to failure. Those aren't Jesus robots down there, they are Frankenstein monsters. And eventually they will turn on the people of God and try to destroy them."

"That's sheer superstition, Joe." Simon was angry. "I helped develop those things. Sometimes I think Jessup may be right when he says your theology is a mixture of Seminole folklore and Greek mythology."

Panther whirled, facing his friend. His eyes were flashing. "Seminole folklore? Listen, Simon, robot religion is always doomed to failure. There is but one Jesus Christ, not 48 Christ's made with wires and transistors. People down there are actually worshiping those mechanical idols...."

Panther paused, catching his breath. He knew his temper was flaring again, knew he had to control it if he was to make his point to father and son who were so new in spiritual things. "Let me tell you about robots," he continued. "The term comes from the Czech word for forced labor and was invented by Karel Capek. It was popularized in his melodrama of 1921, *R.U.R.* In his story, the robots looked and behaved like people, but were built without such impractical attributes as feeling or a soul. They were designed to do all the world's work, wage all the world's wars, and then finally rebel and destroy their makers. Capek was discounted as a mad man and his theories were rejected by the general public. But his principle is not madness, nor does it stem from Seminole folklore; I believe it is spiritual truth.

"When a metal creature feels immortal longings, no mere law can rein him in. Remember the computer in the movie *2001*. His name was HAL. He not only operated the spaceship, but said quite frankly, 'I am incapable of making a mistake.'"

Panther paused. He could feel his heart pounding furiously in his chest. "People are treating those Jesus robots down there as though they are infallible. They are replacing God. And as for your 'God Star' – that DEOSAT – I fully believe it is capable of murder if given a chance."

The two men, Joe Panther and Simon Pedersen, stood facing each other across the table. Mark had risen to his feet also and was looking first at his father, then at the dark-skinned, muscular man with the coal black hair and cowboy clothes. No one spoke for a long minute. Finally Simon Pedersen broke the silence.

"I think you've gone too far, Joe. I'll give it thought, but you need to know I think you're off base and about to get caught in a rundown. Now, if you'll excuse us. I promised Mark to give him a personal tour of Jesus World. I want him to see the Crucifixion, the Resurrection, and the Ascension firsthand."

"My God, Simon, there is but one Crucifixion. Christ died once and for all. There is but one

Resurrection. To keep on replaying it makes that first resurrection a travesty."

Simon Pedersen ignored the Indian's plea. Reaching across the table where Joe was standing, he shook his hand. "I love you deeply, Joe, but if you keep on this way, it will be the end of our friendship. I've left Jesus World, but I still believe in it. Now we've got to go. I'm praying this will be the most important day in Mark's life."

They were gone, leaving Joe alone in the apartment. He stood at the big plate glass window. Far below him, he could see the people streaming, shoving, rushing to get the best places to see the Crucifixion drama. It was 1 p.m., and time to kill Jesus all over again.

The phone in the penthouse was ringing. Joe walked to Simon's desk and picked it up. It was his ranch foreman, the former deputy sheriff.

"Joe, they told me I could find you there. We got big trouble. Jessup drained our catfish pond last night. Now he's got his men out here with a dragline. They're filling it in, saying they are going to turn it into a parking lot for Jesus World."

XIV

IT WAS A PERFECT DAY for the Crucifixion. The temperature was in the lower 80s. The azure blue sky was dotted with white, fluffy clouds. The orange blossoms from the surrounding groves perfumed the air.

Nearly 75,000 people were on hand to see the main event. As an added attraction on this Palm Sunday, the program director at Jesus World had arranged for a Triumphal Entry. A real live Jesus, played by Hollywood's current Oscar winner, rode down the main thoroughfare to the Temple on a live donkey. Members of the Praetorian Guard went before him, passing out small palm branches to those who were closest to the street. The scene was so touching that hundreds of men took off their jackets and spread them on the street in front of the donkey. Women, moved to tears, threw their jewelry in the street in front of the donkey. Shouts of "Hosanna" and "Blessed is He Who comes in the name of the Lord," rang throughout Jesus World.

Then the attention shifted to Calvary and the semiweekly portrayal of the Crucifixion -- beginning with the long walk by the robot Jesus down the Via Dolorosa and climaxing with another robot Jesus being nailed to the cross.

Following the Crucifixion and the

Resurrection, Simon Pedersen and his son made their way through the crowd. Since they had more than an hour before the Ascension, Simon decided to use the time to take Mark through the Temple.

Mark was confused "Dad, I'm sorry but this isn't what I need. This is only a fantasy visit to a kingdom the way we wish it were. This isn't what life is like, this artificial resurrection. I need to touch a man who really did rise from the dead, not some robot made of wires and springs."

"You'll get that at Koinonia Ranch with Joe Panther," his dad said as they stepped up on the moving sidewalk, on their way toward the Sheep Gate of the Temple. "Right now you're getting a crash course on Bible events. Three days in Jesus World is equal to three years in a seminary."

The sidewalk stopped just outside the gate at the Pool of Bethesda. It was here the Arab princess had received her sight a week before. Since that time, two security guards had been posted to keep the people from leaping into the pool when the robot angel came and troubled the waters, or from touching the Jesus robot as he ministered to the man who had been crippled 38 years.

A large sign now hung near the marble portico of the pool which read: *Do not touch Jesus.*

Simon and Mark stepped off the sidewalk to watch the drama which had just begun. They were aware of some kind of disturbance in the crowd behind them, when suddenly an elderly man pushed roughly around them. He was dragging an old woman behind him. She was blind, desperately groping with her free hand as her frantic husband pulled her through the crowd. The security guard saw them coming and tried to edge his way through the tightly packed crowd to block him from pushing past the velvet ropes strung along the spectator area. But the old man was moving too fast. The guard would not have been able to restrain him anyway, for the recklessness resulting from his despair seemed to give him superhuman strength. Shoving at the giant Mark Pedersen who was in his path, the old man pushed him aside as if he were a stalk of wheat in front of a tractor. Startled, Mark looked down at the man's desperate face.

"Jesus!" the man screamed. "Please heal her. Please! Please!"

The robot Jesus continued its conversation with the impotent man robot who lay stretched on a mat on the inlaid marble floor. "Wilt thou be made whole?" he intoned.

"Please!" the desperate man shouted, shoving his blind wife through the ropes at Jesus. "Touch her! Heal her!"

The Jesus robot was mechanically bending over the prone impotent man robot "Rise," he said in classic English diction, his mouth moving in perfect sequence with his words, "take up thy bed, and walk."

Just as the Jesus robot reached out to touch the man, the blind woman, terrified by her husband's desperate shove, stumbled over the other robot stretched out on the floor. Frantically, she flailed with her arms, trying to find something to support herself as she fell. She grabbed hold of the arm of the Jesus robot and held on. As she did, she stripped away his robe, exposing his intricate mechanism of wires, transistors and electronic circuits.

Something was wrong. Before security guards could pull her away, the Jesus robot had short-circuited. The cables, which ran from the computer in his chest along his arms, that transmitted instructions in the form of electric impulses to his hands, touched one of the exposed wires which had been pulled loose by the woman's frantic clawing. In a flash of sparks, a component burned out and, still in his bending position, the Jesus robot began striking the woman with both arms -- powerful, hammering blows. All the time his smiling face kept saying, "Rise, take up thy bed, and walk."

The first blow caught her across the shoulder, sending her sprawling on top of the robot lying on the floor. That machine, in turn, was getting up, his computer responding to the vocal command of the Jesus robot to rise. The woman was caught between the two robots, one trying to get up, the other hovering over her, striking her down with hard blows across her back and head.

Since this particular Jesus robot worked on hydraulic pressure, his perception was controlled by infrared light and ultrasonic sound rather than an outside power force. There was no way to turn the machine off. The woman was being beaten to death in front of 400 witnesses.

The crowd was screaming in panic. Two women fainted. A man leaped over the ropes to try to drag the blind woman free. He was struck behind the ear by the hammering hands of the robot and knocked senseless to the floor. One of the security guards leaped on the robot's back but was flung into the Pool of Bethesda. The woman's husband, now screaming unintelligible phrases, pushed through the ropes and was immediately hammered to the stone floor. His wife, still trapped between the robot that kept rising and lowering and the hammering hands, was no longer screaming. Her crushed body continued to absorb the heavy blows of the robot with sickening sounds. Blood was streaming from her ears and nose. Her sightless eyes stared vacantly into the face of the "savior" as he hammered the last breath of life from her jerking body.

The second security guard finally pushed his nightstick into the mechanism on the chest of the Jesus robot. In a shower of sparks the robot slowly ceased his pounding, stood erect and repeated, over and over, the opening words of his speech -- "Wilt thou be made whole? Wilt thou be made whole? Wilt thou be made whole? Wilt thou...."

Dazed and helpless to do anything, Simon looked up at his son. Mark's face was drained of color. His eyes glassy. "My God, Dad, is this what you've created?"

"Mark, son..." Simon was grasping for words. The medical attendants were pushing their way through the crowd. The dazed security guard had been pulled from the Pool of Bethesda. The words were still coming from the mouth of the Jesus robot, although very faintly now, and slowly, "Wilt...thou...be...made..."

"It's just like Joe Panther said," Mark screamed, looking down at this dad "These things are full of demons. They will turn on us. Destroy us. They've got to be stopped." His voice was raging as he thrashed his head back and forth.

Simon realized what had happened. The awful tragedy played out just feet before them had sent Mark into a flashback. He was no longer in control. Simon reached out to detain him, to try to calm him. But in a powerful reaction his huge, gangly son grabbed him, pinning his arms to his chest, and literally picked him off the ground. Spinning him like a fisherman throws a cast net, he threw him into the crowd. Several men and women were knocked to the floor as Simon crashed into them. Mark, screaming and waving his huge arms in the air like a raging giant, dashed back along the moving sidewalk, which had been brought to an emergency stop because of the tragedy. By the time Simon clambered to his feet, his wild-eyed son had disappeared into the mob of people heading toward the arena where the final countdown for the Ascension was about to begin.

XV

JOE PANTHER, his Indian face set like dark flint, shouldered his way through the late afternoon crowd. For three hours he had been stalking Bert Jessup through the maze of attractions. Every place he had been, Jessup had just left. Fortunately he had not found him earlier, after he had received the phone call from his camp that the pond had been drained, for he would have done what he used to do to men who betrayed him on the rodeo circuit -- in the days before Christ took control of his life. The raging anger had subsided somewhat, but the determination to find Bert Jessup was even stronger.

At one time Joe Panther had been known as an expert tracker. He could easily track down a deer in the Big Cypress Swamp as a boy. Part of his skill had been learned from his Seminole father. But most of it was instinct -- just as he could sense the presence of evil, or danger. Back then, running with soft moccasin shoes through the tall grass of a slough, or moving silently through a hammock on the balls of his feet, he could tell by mashed grass, a tuft of hair on a twig, water oozing from a depression in earth or even the temperature of animal droppings, not only what his quarry looked like but exactly where he was.

But the jungle of Jesus World was different. There were no distinct signs. No unique smells. In the 'Glades everything had its own smell. Here, in this mob, there was no way to distinguish man from animal, even good from evil. He was confused, but he could not leave. He had to confront Jessup.

Panther had never seen so many people. Every race, nationality, every costume on earth seemed represented. He seldom came into Jesus World. The place depressed him. The last time he was here, he - - like the man who had earlier gone crazy in the park -- had to restrain himself from grabbing the whip out of the hands of the Jesus robot who was chasing the moneychangers from the Temple, and use it on the gawking crowd who stood around sighing with ooohhs and aaahhs.

This afternoon it was the crowd who prevented him from finding Jessup. They were swarming like honeybees in a dead cypress tree. Joe could not even see the ground beneath his feet. Twice he was jostled from behind and felt a hand reaching for his wallet in his hip pocket. The second time he slashed with his right hand at the groping fingers, felt the side of his palm crush against a wrist, and heard a scream of pain. But by the time he turned his head, the anguished face he expected to see was gone. There was only that great sea of faces pushing on toward the Mount of Olives arena, their eyes straining to catch a glimpse of any action.

It was only 15 minutes until the automatic countdown from DEOSAT activated the invisible magnetic field for the Ascension. The Praetorian Guard were busy, herding all people out of the danger zone and forming their human chain around the base of the mountain -- arms tightly linked together -- until the magnetic field was activated.

After that no one could get through until DEOSAT sent its all-clear signal.

There was no way Joe could find Jessup in the crowd. Ahead was one of the little way stations scattered throughout the park -- "Samaritan Inns" they were named, recalling the place where the Good Samaritan took his wounded friend in Jesus' story. Inside were restrooms, a small refreshment stand (with a robot innkeeper who responded to vocal commands and served candy bars and cold drinks), and a bank of telephones. Panther headed for the telephones. He had tried to reach Jessup earlier by phone from Simon's apartment, but he had been told he was out in the park. Maybe he had returned by now.

Ironically, the person who answered the phone was a secretary who had formerly worked at Koinonia Ranch. She had remained a close friend of Panther's, keeping him informed of much that was happening behind the scenes at Jesus World.

"Everything has gone wrong today, Joe," she said, her voice quivering. "All the office staff was called back to work. I just learned about the fish pond, but there has been so much else happening. I haven't had time to contact anyone. It's as though Satan himself has taken control."

"What do you mean?" Panther asked, feeling the tiny hairs on his arms beginning to rise. It was a sign he'd almost forgotten, a signal he used to recognize when he would hunt with his Indian cousins in the Everglades and they were approaching danger. Once, when he was crossing a small stream on a log, the hairs on the back of his arms began to rise. He had paused just in time to see a huge cottonmouth moccasin, curled on the log at his feet. Another step and he would have been dead. Now the hairs on his arms were doing the same thing.

The secretary continued. "Officials from the Federal Aviation Administration were out last week. They said our electronic devices are interfering with the instrument approach patterns of planes at the Orlando airport. They claimed two major air crashes have been directly linked to the Second Coming. This morning we received a court order issued on the authority of the FAA, ordering us to cancel all Second Comings until a hearing before a federal judge. The only problem is, we can't control the Second Comings and don't know when the next one will take place. DEOSAT is in control. He might even send a Second Coming tonight, which would mean big trouble, since it would put us in contempt of court.

"Then this afternoon the flood gates that cause the River Jordan to back up, stuck in the open position. This shorted out Elijah's fiery chariot and Prophet Land had to be closed. The concessionaires are angry since no people in Prophet Land means no cold drinks will be sold. The manager at Jonah's Place organized the fast food operators and they are threatening a class action suit against Jessup. The pipefitters union went on strike at noon today, which meant the graves that normally open during the Crucifixion scene were stuck wide open. A man fell into the grave of Elisha and broke his back. Then to top it all, a blind woman was killed at the Pool of Bethesda. Now our monitors have picked up a mad man who has gone crazy in the park and tearing the heads off all the Jesus robots."

"Pray they don't catch him until he finishes his job," muttered Panther to himself. Then more quietly. "I'm sorry you've got so many troubles, but I still need to find Jessup."

"He just came in, Joe. He's back in his office. I'll see if I can get him on the line."

"Don't tell him it's me," Panther said. "Just tell him it's another emergency call."

Jessup's voice sounded on the edge of panic when he came on the line. Joe wasted no time in stating his case.

Jessup listened for only a minute, then he interrupted.

"You're wasting your breath, Indian," Jessup snapped "I've got too many troubles this afternoon to listen to you. Tomorrow I'll deal with your situation."

"What do you mean by that?"

"I mean this morning your friend, Simon Pedersen, resigned from the board of Jesus World. That puts me in charge. Koinonia Ranch now belongs to me. Better start packing, because in a week that ranch of yours will be a parking lot."

Panther was too stunned to counter. "But what about Simon's agreement?"

"Pedersen is out of the picture now." Jessup snorted. "You've been nothing but trouble to me, Panther, and I want you gone."

The phone clicked in Panther's ear. Jessup had hung up.

Mark Pedersen was a wild man. He had smashed his way through the New Testament side of Jesus World, running wildly from one attraction to another, tearing the heads off all the Jesus robots he could find. In the Upper Room he had not only destroyed the Jesus robot, he had turned the Lord's Supper table upside down and short-circuited the entire foot-washing drama in the next room. At Gethsemane he had knocked two men unconscious and then attacked the robot of the Apostle Peter who was about to cut off the electronic ear of the servant of the high priest with his sword.

He intended to hurl the Peter robot into the crowd but did not know he was one of the few robots attached to high voltage wires. He had been badly burned when a high voltage wire fell across his left arm, burning through his shirt sleeve and searing the flesh to the bone. Although the shock had knocked him down, he was still able to grab Peter's sword to behead the two robots sleeping by a tree. He then thrust it into the back of the Jesus robot, still sweating water and blood, causing it to explode in a shower of sparks and smoke. Every place Mark went he left destruction.

The Praetorian Guard, usually on hand to apprehend people who went out of control, were all at the base of the Mount of Olives. The crowd was so great that day they were having trouble restraining them. But the automatic countdown was to begin any minute, and anyone inside the danger zone could be cooked alive by the powerful microwaves which activated the Ascension sequence. Arm in arm, the Praetorian Guard had formed a human fence all the way around the base of the artificial mountain, just outside of where the invisible magnetic barrier would momentarily switch on. At that moment, the security officers would be free to subdue the mad giant who had gone berserk. Until then, however, not a single man could leave his post. It was all they could do to hold back the straining, pressing mob of more than 90,000 people, much less apprehend one drug-crazed maniac who was ripping the heads off the robots.

But the Praetorian Guard did not have to go after Mark Pedersen. He started toward them at almost the same instant his father spotted him.

"Mark, for God's sake, stop!" Simon screamed over the heads of the mass of people as he closed in on his son.

"For God's sake I cannot stop!" the tall, powerful young man panted "This place is evil. I must destroy it. I must warn everyone to get away before the evil kills them."

"Mark," his father panted, "what happened to that blind woman was an accident. An industrial accident. It could happen in any factory. Please, Mark. Let me help you."

But Mark had spotted the Mount of Olives. In his drug-crazed condition, he saw it as the ideal place where he could warn all the people to leave. Powerfully shoving his way through the crowd, pushing people aside and behind, his arms and elbows lifted high over the heads of the shorter men and women, he headed for the base of the Mount of Olives and the human wall of security guards wearing the uniforms of the Roman Praetorian Guard.

They saw him coming and tried to reinforce their grip on each other. But there was no way any of the men could leave his post to back up the ones directly in front of the raging giant with the wavy hair and dark-rimmed glasses. Mark Pedersen, roaring like a charging elephant,

144

crashed headlong into the human fence, sending six men sprawling. Breaking through, he stumbled and fell, clawing at the ground trying to regain his footing so he could head up the hill.

Two of the guards grabbed at his legs. Mark rolled on the ground, his glasses flying into the crowd, and clubbed with those big hands at the arms of the men holding him. He heard the sharp crack of a broken bone and the shrill scream as blood spurted from the arm of one of the security men. Two other men grabbed at his legs, but he twisted and rolled up the hill.

The other men, their arms still linked to hold back the pressing mob, looked on helplessly as Mark kicked the last of his restrainers in the face, knocking his red-plumed helmet high in the air. The man grabbed his face in pain and Mark scrambled to his feet. His left arm, oozing blood from the deep burn, hung helpless at his side as he began running up the steep hill, his long legs churning. He slipped, fell, clambered to his feet and struggled on toward the top of the Mount of Olives.

Trapped in the crowd, Simon Pedersen could not move. For a moment he thought the Praetorian Guard had caught Mark. If they could only hold him until Simon could wedge his way through the people, he was sure he could calm him. Then he saw his son scrambling up the side of the steep hill, stumbling, falling, pumping his legs as he raced toward the top of the grassy knoll.

"Oh, God," Simon choked out, reaching his arms over the shoulders of the crowd in front of him, "please stop him."

The members of the Praetorian Guard were

shouting at Mark -- commanding him, begging him to come down. At any second the magnetic field would be activated. After that no one could reach him, nor could he get out. He would fry like bacon in a skillet when the microwaves touched the top of the mountain.

But Mark was oblivious to all but one thing. He needed to warn the people. Reaching the top of the hill, he stood like a colossus, his feet spread apart, his eyes blinking in the setting sun. Raising his long arms, he cried out in a hoarse voice, "Flee! Flee! This place is evil."

Turning in all directions to face all the people, he repeated his message, over and over.

Suddenly, at the base of the mountain, there was another commotion. The Praetorian Guard were arguing with someone. Shouts went up and then, in a burst of strength, another man smashed through the human fence. Unlike the gangly Mark Pedersen, he did not fall. Running on the balls of his feet, his coal black hair catching the glint of the setting sun, Joe Panther raced up the steep side of the Mount of Olives. He bounded like a key deer through the Big Cypress Swamp, like a black panther racing after quarry, like his ancestors had run through the high grass of the Everglades. His motion was effortless, his muscular legs driving him to the top where he hoped to grab the young son of his old friend and carry him to the base of the mountain and safety.

The crowd grew silent as they saw what was happening. But despite all Joe Panther's strength, he was no match for the man giant at the top of the hill.

"For God's sake," Joe said as he stood

dwarfed before Mark, "and for your dad's
sake...."

Mark, staring wildly beyond Panther at the
red ball of the setting sun, suddenly swung his
good right arm, catching Panther full across the
chest. Joe lost his balance and began rolling
down the steep hill. A huge gasp went up from
the crowd.

Suddenly there was a loud click, and the
magnetic field turned on. Joe Panther, tumbling
down the hill, was stopped abruptly by the invisible
fence. Realizing what had happened, he also
realized the countdown sequence had begun. In that
split second, he made a decision. He could have
stayed at the base of the hill, crouched against the
invisible fence, and perhaps been safe from the
microwaves which would descend at any minute.
Clambering back to his feet, his face and hands
bleeding from the abrasions, he started back up the
hill.

It was not until he started to move that he
realized his left leg was broken.

The pain was so intense he momentarily
blacked out, collapsed and fell back against the
invisible fence. Recovering, he reached down and
felt the bone poking through the skin just above the
knee. It was a compound fracture, and his pants
were soaked with blood. Putting his hands over the
splintered protrusion, he could feel the blood
pumping from the wound. The jagged bones had
severed an artery.

Simon Pedersen had made his way through the
crowd toward Joe Panther. He looked at the
Indian's useless leg and shouted, "Don't try it, Joe.
Take your belt and make a tourniquet. There's no

way to save Mark now. Save yourself."

Joe Panther looked down at Simon Pedersen, smiled slightly, and shook his head. Then rolling over on his stomach, Joe started the long crawl back up to the top of the Mount of Olives.

XVI

MARK PEDERSEN, standing in a daze on the top of the Mount of Olives, suddenly leaped back. A trap door had sprung open almost immediately beneath his feet. A huge, eight-foot Jesus robot, dressed in a glittering white robe, appeared out of an underground silo. Brilliant floodlights flashed on automatically as the smiling robot, his glass eyes glittering, raised his arms over the crowd.

The arena became silent as the rumbling voice of the robot floated out over the heads of the spectators.

"It's not for you to know the times or the seasons which the Father hath put in his own power...."

"Lies!" shouted Mark Pedersen. Now it was he who was dwarfed by the huge Jesus beside him. "He's a fake. He's not real!"

The Jesus robot continued to smile, his arms extending in a divine blessing over the people below. "But ye shall receive power, after that the Holy Ghost is come upon you: and ye shall be witnesses unto me...."

"He's false. He's plastic," Mark screamed at the crowd. Even his blood is artificial. He's not alive. Look!"

Frantically Mark began tearing at the giant Jesus, wildly ripping at the arms, at his robe.

"He's all wires," Mark shouted hoarsely, using

his good right hand to twist the long arm which
extended out over the crowd. The arm bent at a
crazy angle, then snapped loose, exposing an
intricate connection of wires, springs and cables.
Sparks shot from the broken shoulder joint where
the arm dangled useless. "See, he's not real. He's
just a robot. He can't save you."

Sobbing, screaming, he tore at the huge plastic
figure beside him. He pulled at the head, twisting
the neck until the head drooped grotesquely. More
wires were exposed. More sparks showered the top
of the hill.

"Ye shall be baptized with the Holy Spirit not
many days from now," the robot slurred, his mouth
uttering the words although his head was bent and
hanging far over one shoulder.

Mark ripped at the seamless robe, trying
desperately to claw open the chest and get at the
rectenna inside. The robot, in a ghostly fashion,
continued to turn, its one good arm still moving in a
blessing over the stunned crowd at the base of the
hill.

Joe Panther, crawling in the shadows, leaving a
streak of dark red blood behind him on the grass,
had finally reached the summit.

"Mark!" he shouted from his prone position on
his stomach, his voice intense with pain. "Please,
Mark! Come down from the hill. Leave it in God's
hands. You don't have to conquer evil by force.
'Vengeance is mine, I will repay, says the Lord.'"

"I can't help it, Joe," Mark shouted frantically,
still ripping at the badly crippled robot Jesus.
"Someone has to stamp out this evil."

"Mark, the battle is already won. You don't
have to defend the true Christ. He is victor despite
what men do to His image."

"Go away, Joe. Leave me alone."

Grabbing hold of the other side of the robot Jesus, Joe Panther painfully pulled himself erect. The leg of his trousers was soaked with blood. The splintered bone had ripped through the cloth and was protruding, a sickly white against the crimson stain.

"Please, Joe," Mark was weeping. "Don't make me hit you again."

Then, like Samson of old, Panther's strength returned. Reaching out, he grabbed the young giant with his powerful arms. Both feet planted firmly on the top of the Mount of Olives, he slowly raised the flailing man over his head and in a superhuman show of strength, threw him down the side of the mountain.

Suddenly, at that very instant, the entire top of the mountain glowed in an eerie, ethereal light. It was the "Shekinah." The countdown was over. DEOSAT was in control. The beam locked on target, effusing the mountain top in the golden green light.

The microwaves entered Joe Panther's body from every direction, instantly transforming each cell from solid matter to gas. For a long second his body glowed as the intense heat of the electromagnetic waves evaporated his cellular structure. The glow continued, then disappeared as the semi-weekly blinding flash of light covered the top of the mountain.

As the stunned spectators watched from below, their eyes riveted on the unearthly drama taking place before them, the mutilated figure of Jesus emerged from the top of the light. His left arm was dangling around his knees, ripped loose at the shoulder. His robe was ripped, exposing springs and wires hanging loose from his side. His head tilted crazily over on one shoulder, exposing the wires which led to the rectenna in his torso. The photoelectric process of the Ascension continued.

As the distorted robot image slowly ascended, a great gasp went up from the crowd below. Following after him, just inches below, was the holographic image of Joe Panther, his body now molecularized by fission. Side by side, the two images, the robot Jesus disfigured and shattered by Mark Pedersen's wild attack and the molecularized image of the dead Joe Panther following just below, rose into the sky in a grotesque ascension.

From the bottom of the hill, Mark Pedersen, his hair singed and his clothes smoldering from the peripheral effects of the microwaves, watched in stunned reality as the two images rose slowly into the darkening sky. Six miles above the earth, the final rays of the setting sun caught both figures which had grown big enough to fill a quadrant of the sky. There was a smile on Panther's face, and easily seen was the image of his Greek New Testament in his cowboy shirt pocket.

Then, as the images rose higher, the sky suddenly exploded into a kaleidoscope of color. First the rainbow, then flashes of lightning, and finally the great northern lights of the *aurora borealis.* The figures were gone.

Mark tried to stand to his feet, but his legs were too weak. Looking at the top of the Mount of Olives, he saw where the trap door had closed on the broken torso of the Jesus robot which had been too bent out of shape to return to its hidden silo. The body of Joe Panther was nowhere in sight. It had been totally consumed by the powerful microwaves from the devil in the sky -- DEOSAT.

Suddenly the sky was again filled with light. Looking up, Mark saw the images of the angels descending. Hovering over the horrified crowd, they chanted their weekly litany.

"Ye men of Galilee, why stand ye gazing up into heaven? This same Jesus, which is taken up from you into heaven, shall so come in like manner...."

Mark bent his head to the earth, weeping. His hands were wet, slippery on the grass. He looked at them as the ethereal light faded from the heavens. They were covered with blood. He was lying in the same spot where Joe Panther had broken his leg. He was covered in the blood of the man who had died that he might live.

A loud bell rang, indicating the magnetic field had been shut off. Mark felt a hand on his shoulder. He looked up into the tear-stained face of his father.

"Let's go home, son," Simon said quietly. "It's all over."

XVII

THE DESTRUCTION of Koinonia Ranch by
Bert Jessup's earth movers was even more
complete than the devastation of Jerusalem by
the Roman Emperor Titus in 70 A.D. At least
Titus did not pave over Jerusalem, turning it into
a parking lot for tour buses. But that is exactly
what Jessup did to the ranch.

Of course, Bert Jessup did it in a most
humane way. There was a special service for Joe
Panther, with eulogies from many celebrities.
The families living on the ranch were given
plenty of time to move and sell their cattle
before the bulldozers and asphalt machines
arrived.

Before the end of June the ranch had ceased
to exist. Several pastors on Jessup's advisory
board wanted to put a memorial plaque at the
gate. It seemed they should do something to
honor Joe Panther, who had planted more than
two decades of his soul in the rich, black earth
below the asphalt. One of the men suggested
they could at least put up a bronze marker
calling it the "Joe Panther Memorial Tour Bus
Parking Lot." In the press of other business, the
idea was dropped.

For five days after the double tragedy, Jesus
World had been shut down for repairs. A team of
computer experts had been brought in to
straighten out Golem and recheck the DEOSAT

154

operation. The damaged Jesus robots were replaced, new security measures worked out, and additional guards put on the staff. The FAA suit was settled through a costly new system of computer controls.

Jesus World would have gone bankrupt without the Arab deal. It had taken days of negotiation with the highest ranking leaders in the Moslem world. But they had finally agreed to put up the money to save Jesus World. In return, Jessup agreed to build a super attraction dedicated to Islam.

But the Arabs no longer wanted Mohammed to appear in the Second Coming. Instead, they asked Jessup to recreate Mt. Moriah, the second most holy place in Islam. To do it right, the Garden of Gethsemane -- where it all began -- had to be eliminated. But the Arab sheiks were pleased with the new attraction. Every hour on the hour, true to Moslem tradition, a robot Mohammed flew across the sky above Jesus World on a winged horse from Mecca, touching down on top of Mt. Moriah.

Simon Pedersen saw to it himself that the remnants of Panther's followers were properly taken care of. Most of the men returned to their previous jobs, carrying out the work of the ministry the best they could. It was Simon who seemed out-of-pocket-uncomfortable about returning to the corporate life, yet uncertain just where he belonged.

"Find out who you are," Panther had said to him that fateful afternoon so long ago when he had appeared on Simon's front porch to interrupt his planned suicide. "Find out who you are, then put aside everything else and go after it."

Simon also remembered a morning teaching session back at Koinonia Ranch. The men were in the lodge, seated in a semicircle around Joe Panther. "Suppose you are the wealthiest man in the world," Panther had challenged the group, "and you have three years to win the world to God. How would you do it?"

There had been various suggestions from the group. One man thought it best accomplished by a television hookup through a satellite which would beam the message of salvation to all the world at once. Another had insisted it start with the political leaders of the world. Bring all the heads of state together, he had said, and win them to God. Still another wanted to get all the church leaders together. Others had urged social reforms, feeding the hungry, building houses for the poor. Simon remembered he had suggested building Jesus World.

Joe had listened patiently, then advised them to look at how Jesus had done it. In three years.

"He did not move from Nazareth to Rome and set up headquarters. He never sought out a political or religious leader. He did not have a campaign director, or a booking agent. Instead of seeking publicity, He told many of the people He healed to tell no man.

"Jesus chose 12 men and poured His life into them. In the end He breathed on them and told them, 'receive the Holy Spirit.' After He ascended the Holy Spirit arrived, and those same men went out and performed miracles identical to Jesus."

Then Joe had asked the question -- the same question Simon had asked Bert Jessup that night on the Bahaman beach -- "Has anyone improved on the method of Jesus? Jesus gathered a small group around Him, poured His life into them, then told them to go and do likewise -- imparting the Holy Spirit as they went."

Simon Pedersen knew that commission was still in effect. He was to be a fisher of men. That meant returning to the *Marah* with a small group of men -- including his son, Mark. He would use the ship as Jesus used the fishing boats on the Sea of Galilee -- to impart his life, to impart the Holy Spirit, into the lives of a few. He would take up the task left unfinished by Jesus, unfinished by Joe Panther, building men.

Simon's final meeting with Bert Jessup took place at a table in the Celestial City Restaurant atop David's citadel, high above Jesus World. It was a hot Monday morning in July, an hour before the restaurant opened to the public. The two men sat at a table in front of one of the big windows, drinking coffee. Only the chefs and waiters were present, preparing for the 300 people who would soon come up the Sky-vators to eat lunch and enjoy the panorama from the rotating restaurant.

"I took a final walk through Jesus World last night," Simon told Jessup. "It was sad. I see you've added an attraction to honor the Unification Church."

"The Moonies made me a deal I couldn't refuse," Jessup said. "They are donating more than a thousand acres of ranchland on the other side of the Interstate. We're going to start work on All Faiths World within the year. It could be even bigger than Jesus World. Christians need to know what the Hindus and Buddhists believe also. It will draw people of all religions from all over the world."

"I know," Simon said "Once you get them here, you'll expose them to Jesus."

"Of course, Simon," Bert replied 'That's why we're in business. Not to make money, but to lead people to Jesus."

Simon looked sadly at his old friend, Bert Jessup. In recent weeks he had let his hair grow long and then had it styled in an Afro. It seemed out of proportion to his chubby body and quivered when he was agitated. The pudgy index finger on his right hand sported a two-carat diamond ring -- a gift from an Arab oil sheik with whom he had recently struck up a friendship. He was wearing a $700 suit, and his Gucci alligators glistened under the table.

A vacuum cleaner was running in the background as a janitor finished cleaning the carpet before the customers arrived. The huge motor which rotated the restaurant had not been switched on, so the platform on which the two men sat was stationary, almost directly over the Gate Beautiful of the Temple. Below, Simon could see the robots Peter and John healing the man who had been crippled from birth. Even from that altitude he could hear the shouts of praise and exclamation as the robot stood erect and then went walking and leaping into the Temple area.

"Tell me, Bert," Pedersen said, slowly sipping his coffee as he looked through the huge slanted windows at the crowds below, "with all your attractions from the Bible, why didn't you ever depict the scene in the Upper Room?"

"But we did. We show the Lord's Supper there."

"No, I don't mean that Upper Room. I mean the Upper Room in Acts 1:13 where the 120 gathered on the Day of Pentecost"

"Simon, we can't have all the Bible scenes, you know. We've just picked the most significant for Jesus World."

"It's interesting," Pedersen mused, looking down at the Gate Beautiful where the robot beggar continued to praise God for his healing. "Anyone can artificially create a miracle. Cecil B. deMille opened the Red Sea in his spectacular film *The Ten Commandments* and you resurrect Jesus twice a week. But no man can create the power of Pentecost -- not even Yosef Ben-Korach. That's the reason you didn't build an Upper Room. Everything else can be imitated, but Pentecost is personal. You cannot remain a spectator when you are exposed to the power of the Holy Spirit."

"I don't like the way you put that," Jessup said. "We've tried to present the gospel."

"Well, I've got to say it. Joe Panther said it too, and Jesus World killed him."

"Wait a minute, Simon. I never intended for it to come to that." For a brief moment Bert's eyes softened.

"It came to that," Pedersen said, clipping his words, "the moment you took your eyes off the risen Christ and fastened them on a robot. That's the reason you don't need the Holy Spirit at Jesus World. You're plugged into the Florida Power and Light Company. What you call miracles are no more than the black magic of Pharaoh's magicians. What they did with magic, you do with electronics. But, as Mark says, it's all plastic. These people out here need more than a fake Jesus on a Styrofoam cross. They need a relationship with the Spirit of God. A visit to

Jesus World is like making love to a robot. All the senses are there -- sound, smell, taste, sight, feel. But when you're finished with your lovemaking, the machine clicks off and you're left alone with nothing but transistors and wires. There is no relationship. No love. That's the missing ingredient around here. Love. It's an ingredient which can only be provided by the Holy Spirit. All you've done is drape the robe of Jesus over the shoulders of the world system."

"Won't you ever understand, Simon?" Jessup said calmly. "Thousands of people are being saved here every day."

"It's not robots that save people, Bert, it is the power of the Holy Spirit. If the same spirit that raised Christ from the dead dwells in you, He will quicken your mortal body. That cannot be done through electronics -- only through a relationship. And that's the reason I am leaving and will never return to this place."

Bert Jessup leaned back, gently blowing air through puffed cheeks. Simon could almost sense his feeling of relief.

"What are your plans, Simon?"

"There are a group of men waiting for me now in Ft. Pierce -- twelve of them to be exact. Two are leftovers from Koinonia Ranch. The rest are young men from the business world. One of them is my son, Mark. We're sailing this afternoon on the *Marah*. I don't know how long we'll be gone -- at least until I have had a chance to do for them what Joe Panther did for me."

Bert Jessup, glancing at his watch, stood. "I have to go," he said. "The attorney for the Moonies has flown in from Korea. They will be making the first major contribution to all Faiths

World. We've got to lift our vision. The world is bigger than any of us ever dreamed."

Simon Pedersen settled hack in his chair and reached for his coffee cup. "You're a tortured man, Bert. A deceived man. What began as something beautiful has become a nightmare. It may last for a while, for the mills of God grind slowly, but eventually it will fall."

Jessup was standing. He shook Pedersen's hand and disappeared into the waiting angel capsule of the Sky-vator. "Goodbye, Simon. May God bless you."

"Goodbye, Bert," Pedersen said softly as the doors of the Sky-vator swished closed "May God *forgive* you."

XVIII

THE MOON over Grand Bahama Island was at half crescent, almost directly overhead. The beach was quiet at West End. Near the long stone jetty which extended out into the sea, a group of men sat on the sand. Their leader, an aging man with bronzed face under a tousled thatch of silver hair; was sitting on a piece of coquina rock under a cluster of coconut palms. The group of men, all dressed in cut-offs and tennis shoes, had their backs to the gently rolling surf, listening intently as the older man talked. To their left, far down the beach, an ancient stern-wheeler strung with gaudy light bulbs was tied to the end of a rickety dock. Behind them, across the Gulf Stream, was the mainland of Florida. The only sound, other than the gentle lapping of the water on the white sand beach, was the rustle of the wind in the palms and the low voice of the teacher as he spoke earnestly to his companions.

"You do well to remember the scuba diving lessons you received this afternoon when we were fishing for lobster and conch. You discovered a man can live underwater in a foreign environment, but the rules are different. The first principle of underwater survival is you cannot live underwater using above-water rules.

"The same is true in the Kingdom of God.

There are two worlds -- the natural world and the spiritual world. Paul told the Corinthians, 'The natural man cannot understand the things of the Spirit of God, for they are foolishness to him.'

"The new Christian must be trained like a diver with tanks. If he does not know how to use his equipment, he will drown. He must learn how to function in another realm, using a different set of principles."

"I guess that means," one of the men spoke up -- a tall, gangly black-headed giant with dark-rimmed glasses, "that we should not try to run the Kingdom of God by the rules that govern politics and industry."

The silver-haired man grinned at his son. The seeds were taking root. He looked down at his own feet. His tennis shoes were off and he enjoyed digging his toes in the warm sand of the beach. It was good to be free, the kind of freedom that comes from accepting the truth.

"When Jesus ascended into heaven," the leader said softly, his eyes focusing on one man in the group, then another, "He did not give His followers instructions to build a kingdom. Rather, He told them to wait on the person of the Holy Spirit. The Spirit, coming in great power, anointed each man with a personal Pentecost. He enabled each one of them to find his place in the Body of Christ and gave each one special gifts to edify the Body. Jesus said He needed to leave so the Spirit could come. He is still coming, this Holy Spirit, empowering us, giving us knowledge, giving us the boldness to die if necessary, that the gospel might spread to all nations."

The men sat quietly, letting the words sink in. The soft, tropical breeze fanned their faces, ruffled their hair. The water splashed against the rocks to their right, ebbing and flowing as the waves exerted their constant pressure. Had it not been for the electric lights far down the beach, this could have been another group of men sitting on the shore of a Galilean sea, listening as another Teacher spoke gentle truths about the Kingdom of His Father.

One day soon, however, they would return to their jobs in the secular world -- including Mark Pedersen, who would go back into the world of business to bring to it what he was learning. But for now, he was sitting like the rest, cross-legged in the soft sand, his knees propped up near his chest, supporting his arms where he rested his huge head.

"Dad, does Jesus still heal?" he asked

"Jesus is the same yesterday, today and forever. He still heals. The same Holy Spirit who lived in the man Jesus now lives in those of us who make up the Body of Christ. 'The things that I do, ye shall do also,' Jesus told His disciples. 'In fact, ye shall do even greater things because I go to my Father.'"

"Do you think 'greater things' means something like Jesus World?" one of the men asked.

The leader smiled and shook his head. "You don't need the Holy Spirit to operate Jesus World. No, I think Jesus was talking about something at a far deeper level. He was pointing out that as long as He was on earth, the Holy Spirit's power would be limited to Him -- or to those He breathed on physically. But if He left, the Spirit could come to all men. Instead of there being one Jesus, limited to the region of Galilee, there would be millions -- all over the earth -- making up the Body of Christ. The command He gave His first disciples would no longer be limited to those 12, but it would be for us all: *As you go, preach, saying, the kingdom of*

*heaven is at hand. Heal the sick, cleanse the lepers,
raise the dead, cast out devils: freely ye have
received, freely give."*

"Does that mean we, through Jesus, have the
power to do all those things?" Mark asked

"That's what it means," the leader smiled.

"Then can Jesus heal this burn on my arm?"
Mark pulled back the sleeve of the football jersey
he was wearing, exposing the angry red burn he had
received when he tussled with the robot of the
Apostle Peter in the Garden of Gethsemane. He had
been treated by doctors, but the high voltage wires
had burned his arm to the bone. Infection had set in.
The wound was still oozing pus and throbbing with
pain.

"Have you asked Him to heal it?" the leader
asked.

The young man stammered. "I didn't know I
could."

"Then let's ask Him now. As His representative
I'm going to touch you, just as Jesus touched the
sick when He was on earth. I believe He wants to
heal you."

The men moved around on the sand, forming a
circle around the gangly young man who sat in their
midst, his head resting on his knees, his eyes closed.
The men were smiling at each other, laughing, as
though it were the most natural thing in the world to
ask Jesus for a miracle.

"He's alive, you know," the leader said
kneeling down in front of his son. "Jesus is alive,
seated with God in heavenly places. His Spirit is
here with us on this beach."

He reached out to touch Mark's arm with his
fingers. Suddenly the entire western sky burst into
light with an explosion of color. The light started

high in the heavens and descended until it touched the earth, swirling in a brilliant, fascinating array of color. Even the moon at half crescent paled in comparison to the brilliance.

The men turned, drawn away from their prayers, fascinated by what was happening. The reflection of the light, golden green in color, danced across the water, casting shadows on the top of each little wavelet. It took the men by surprise. Startled, they looked at each other, then at their leader.

His face was sad. Once again the real work of the Holy Spirit had been diverted by that which was artificial. DEOSAT had activated the monthly Second Coming at Jesus World, more than 150 miles away.

High in the clouds appeared the figure of Jesus dressed in luminous white, riding a white horse. As he descended, other figures joined him from the clouds, falling in rank behind him. There was a long row of angels, stretching from horizon to horizon. Behind them were the other images: popes, martyrs, apostles, kings, scholars. There were three men dressed in traditional Arab dress, with robes and kaffiyehs. There was a Hindu guru, wrapped in an orange dhoti, between John Wesley and what seemed to be a giant image of Buddha.

The men on the beach began to laugh quietly. Shaking their heads, they turned back to the little task at hand. Miracles, they seemed to understand, did not come from satellites but from God. Hands still clasped around the two figures in the center of the circle, they dropped their heads and began to pray, saying quiet "amens" to the words and actions of the silver-haired man who was filling an apostolic role. Gently Simon laid his hand over the wound on his son's arm.

"In the name of the risen Christ, and in the power of the Holy Spirit, I speak healing to this wound."

He slowly withdrew his hand. The men in the circle, some kneeling, some still sitting on the sand, leaned forward. Looking. Slowly the open wound closed. Then there began appearing the pinkness of new flesh -- tender, but whole. Gone was the ugly oozing burn.

"To God goes the glory," the silver-haired leader said.

Quietly the men once again bowed their heads. Some faces were wet with tears. The young giant in the center of the circle had risen to his feet, towering over the other men, his arms raised, his shadow from the light in the western sky spreading across the entire beach. Tears of thanksgiving flowed down his face.

From high in the heavens came the faint rumble of distant thunder, heralding the monthly arrival of the artificial Christ. But the men heard it not. They had tasted from a spring of living water, had heard the voice of God, had seen the demonstration of His power, and their ears were tuned to another sound. The word came, not through earthquake, wind, or fire but in a still, small voice: "Follow *me*, and I will make you fishers of men."

"If you love me, Simon, feed my sheep."

Jesus World

Jamie Buckingham

For more writings and materials by Jamie Buckingham please visit www.JamieBuckinghamMinistries.com